Also by Paul Pinn –

The Pariah

       - Time Bomb Publishing

Scattered Remains

       - Tanjen Ltd

A small percentage of **The Horizontal Split** includes reworked versions of the last two stories in **Scattered Remains**, namely *The Day of the Muffled Oar* –

Exceptional - *Lawrence Dyer*
Great atmosphere, very believable - *Ray Avery*
The description is excellent. You are there - *Chico Kidd*
Full of dirt, death and insanity. I like it - *Dave Logan*

and *When the Hooghly Screams* –

Brilliant – *Rhys Hughes*
Excellent – *Shaun Jeffrey*
Dostoyevskian – *Roger Keen*

plus *A Cage of Silver Serpents* –

Good atmosphere, lushly described – *Fantasy Tales*
Haunting....vivid....carefully wrought – *Dagon*

originally published in 'Visions' in 1998 and then republished in 'Oktobyr 98'.

THE HORIZONTAL SPLIT

Paul Pinn

A
Time Bomb
Publication

TBP

The Day of the Muffled Oar © 1992
When the Hooghly Screams © 1993
A Cage of Silver Serpents © 1998

First published in Great Britain in the year 2000
by Time Bomb Publishing

ISBN: 0-9539300-1-7

Printed and bound in Great Britain by Proprint,
Old Great North Road, Stibbington, Cambs, PE8 6LR

British Library Cataloguing in Publication Data.
A catalogue record for this book is available from
the British Library.

Time Bomb Publishing
P.O.Box 3061
South Croydon
Surrey
CR2 7ZT

Dedicated to –

The trio who attended an Eltham day centre thirty years ago: the schizophrenic man whose haunted face I can still picture; the paranoid whose happiness at securing employment after treatment is almost as powerful in memory as it was in reality; and Michael, a man with the mind of a child who composed poetry some current poets would be hard pressed to equal

Ronald, a superb drummer and vocalist whose potential was never realized due to schizophrenia triggered by discovering his father in a bedroom, just after he'd blown his brains out with a shotgun

A girl first encountered in a Chiswick pub, who ate chalk, used blackcurrant juice on her face, sounded like an acid casualty, warned of peptosyphilis, played with knives, and eventually burned down her mother's house

Mike, a paranoid schizophrenic, who one impulsive day flew from Canada to Greece and without warning called on an old girlfriend he hadn't seen for six years, hoping to re-establish the relationship; unfortunately her husband wasn't too happy with the idea

The man who stood in the same Acton shop doorway at the same time every morning and carried out The Ritual. First he'd fiddle with his sunglasses, inspecting them, shifting them about on his nose. Then he'd check his walkman, its position in his jacket pocket, the wire connecting it to the headphones. Then he'd fiddle with the headphones in the same manner that he fiddled with his sunglasses. Next he'd check the plastic bag he always carried, as if making sure nothing had fallen out. Concurrent with all this he'd be checking the street and chain-smoking, often getting his cigarette tangled up in the wire. After consulting his wristwatch a few times he'd move off, walking with a slight backward slant

and the countless others.........some nameless, some not

I gave love to Mother Earth in rain to feel her muddy kiss on your cold skin. The winter sog of leafy hair is the wet stroke of grassy fur on the rough bark of her lungs. The pain is giving as trees fuck and fill the mouth with star shit. You can't scream covered with earth and Mother's cold empty night hisses. You hear the call of forest, the shriek of mother crows and future fathers as they rape her mind over again, fill her with poisonous neurosperm as they rip babies from her gut and burn them in furnace fires and motor cars and spread their ashes in the piss pot sky. Truth hurts but she's got to do it before the bastards do it to her again. She's not going to die like one of your fucking animals.

Sarah Donaldson, during a bad yet prophetic moment

1

PSYCHOCRYPTIC OVERLOAD

Two miles from school to home and Sarah Donaldson ran all the way, legs molten, lungs full of the sky. She felt superhuman, unstoppable, capable of anything. She was God, the Devil, the Alien. She was pure predatory genius. Until, that is, she arrived home and realized she'd left her front door keys at school, in her bag in the enemy camp where people laughed behind her back. Well, they wouldn't laugh now she'd smashed up a classroom. Nor would they make their presence felt no matter where she was. Or ensure that whatever she did was never good enough. Jesus Christ, she was a talented individual, almost an adult, and all they wanted to do was choke the life out of her. Turn her into a husk. If she owned a gun she'd shoot them all, like they did in America. Now her guardians had sealed the sanctuary, revealing yet another facet of their hypocrisy.

She picked up a handful of gravel, threw it at the door. It was aimed at her parents, retaliation for the betrayal she felt for being locked out. It did nothing to reduce her anger, only encouraged the monster of blind confusion that lurked within her to once again come to the surface, shake the last of sanity's grave soil from its polymorphous cloak, and with tentacles of inflamed nerve tissue, twist Sarah's pretty face into an ugly mask.

"Bastards," she shouted. "Shut me out and let me in or I'll get in."

She swooped to pick up more gravel, saw small rocks edging a flower border running from the door to a corner of the house. Above them stood large glass eyes, and resenting

1

the way they stared at her, and knowing they were feeding images direct into her parents' brains, Sarah picked up a rock and threw it at the closest eye. It merely blinked with a large crack. She threw another, harder this time, and the eye received it and never gave it back. Undeterred, she threw a third, fourth and fifth, the eye losing its lens and sprouting jagged teeth around its socket. Sarah smashed off the teeth with another rock, entered the eye, found herself in the downstairs toilet, and immediately smelt Old Man's Cock.

"Some Alzheimer's been here infecting your mother," said a gruff voice. "Should cut his dick off and stuff it down his throat."

"Stuff it down his throat like a ferret," said another.

"He is a ferret," added a third.

Sarah rushed into the hallway, screamed, "Where are you? Where you hiding?"

Her voices answered in a rush - *here - there - everywhere you dare - go - in the house - the garden - the bathroom - bedroom - bathroom - bedroom - bathroom - bedroom -*

Sarah darted into the lounge, hands over her ears, screaming for the voices to stop.

- stop what? - the silence - the music - what music? - her music - it's shit -

She punched the stereo on, rammed in one of her father's CDs, tried several times to get it to play. When her voices mocked her she picked up the entire unit, shook it, slammed it back down. The voices continued, but miraculously Eric Clapton's guitar slipped from the speakers and spoke to her in whispers. Sarah wasn't impressed, and the stereo smashed the glass coffee table, the impact a tornado of noise more aggravating than Clapton's guitar or the voices now shouting at her from behind the furniture. Determined to silence them she chased through the lounge, overturning the sofa, armchairs, side tables; bringing down a display cabinet as she checked behind it; emptying a cocktail cabinet on the carpet;

pulling down shelving and curtains until finally turning the television on its back and shattering its square black eye with the video.

"Come out you bastards," she shouted as she peered inside. "I know you're in there." She stuck in her hand and felt around, yelling as glass teeth ripped her skin. Her hand emerged scratched and bloody and looked nothing like it had a moment before.

"What have you done with my hand?" she shouted into the television. "Give it back you bastards, otherwise - ."

- the wise - she's not wise - give it back - front - give it up - what have you done -

"GO AWAY!"

- go away she said - she wants to go away - should she go? - she doesn't know - dirty bitch - where you going? - daddy's study - going to find us - going to smash us up -

Sarah wrecked her father's study, ransacked the kitchen, searched every bedroom, left on every tap so the voices couldn't hide in them. But the voices remained: taunting, repeating, questioning, answering, shrieking discordantly like a flock of harpies trapped in her ears, in her head, in every room, nook, cranny and crack in the house until she stormed into her bedroom, put on headphones, jacked into her special taped compilation, and turned the volume up to near maximum.

The hardcore dance beat of rock-rave Goan mysteries, the inchoate emotion of L7 and Lard, Rubicon and Handsome, the guitar-gutburn of Mindfunk and Soundgarden, the psycho-sexual evisceration of Nine Inch Nails, the dark needle-poxed underbelly of hypnotic-psychotic Ministry, and beyond into the Slovakian brutality of thrash-frenzy Bestialit and Dehydrated - Fuckland and Burnt - and didn't she know it - metal napalm, all fuelling the great onslaught that wiped her voices off the inside of her skull and buried them as mutilated crochets and quavers somewhere deep in her brain.

For forty-five minutes the only voices she heard were meant to be heard, and when she took off the headphones there was only the ringing of eardrum concussion. To celebrate her victory she sorted through her collection of acrylics and oils, cans and brushes, intending to paint a very special picture. She selected a canvas, paced for inspiration, stared at her reflection in the mirror and decided to paint it. No sooner had she selected the colours than a better idea occurred to her.

She painted her face and hands with acrylics, found several spray cans of gold, silver, metallic red and blue, and tried her hand at graffiti on the walls and ceiling of her bedroom, and out on the landing, and downstairs in the hall and lounge, and outside on the double garage doors, with a final flourish on the lawn before the cans emptied.

To gain a better perspective on the lawn design, Sarah climbed a cherry tree near the front wall and sat on a thick branch. At first she saw a fireball, then the core of a thermonuclear explosion, followed by a hugely magnified drop of liquid metal from the planet Vulcan where the star signal came from. Lastly her imagination played a horrid trick on her and she thought she saw a police car. When it stopped by the front door and a WPC got out, followed by a man, Sarah realized it wasn't a trick and settled back to watch them.

They gazed at the garage doors, at the lawn, at each other, then stepped cautiously through the open front door without saying a word. After a minute or an hour Sarah spotted the policeman looking out of her bedroom window. He looked directly at her then turned away as though talking to the woman. Within seconds they appeared and marched up the driveway, cutting across to the tree only when beyond the lawn graffiti. Sarah stiffened, merged with the branch, became part the tree.

"Are you Sarah Donaldson from Hawkdene Girls School?" asked the policewoman.

Sarah didn't respond.

"Can you climb down, please."

Sarah didn't move.

"If you think you're part of the tree and we can't see you, I'm afraid you're wrong."

Sarah didn't believe her, and said so.

"Have I got to climb up there and get you?" said the man.

"No," Sarah shouted down at him. "This tree must not be contaminated at any cost."

She climbed down easily, tried to run off into the road. It was a half-hearted bit of fun and the policeman caught her easily. He handcuffed her and they walked back to the police car. The WPC helped her into the back, sat beside her as the constable called in a progress report on his radio. Sarah thought of a nanny she once had, pictured the two of them playing on the front lawn. The picture merged with a puppy that came and went like so much in her life. No one, not even animals, stayed with her long enough to understand her. All interest was bogus.

An enormous wave of despair crashed over her. She broke into a sweat, felt herself shrinking into the seat, becoming less than insignificant. The WPC asked if she was okay. Sarah nodded automatically, mind spiralling down into a dark pit where images and thoughts could no longer be manufactured.

Another car arrived with two policemen to safeguard the house. Sarah was taken to the local police station and seen by a duty doctor while attempts were made in conjunction with her school to track down her parents, Janet and Bill, mummy killer cow and the money bucket man.

Sarah smiled. What a laugh it had all been - in retrospect, of course. No real laugh at the time, though, all those years ago. Like now, really. No laughter at 35,000 feet. No sleep, either, on the flight line from Paris to Ho Chi Min City. Not with the last transmission received from the star signal to think about, its biochemical imagery too instructive to release.

She was in an Indian restaurant with Asian friends - did she have any? Or was she going to find some? The time was yesterday, the year before, perhaps even tomorrow. They were seated at a table with a surface of water on which bobbed a golden boat holding a tiny doll that looked like her. Bigger black boats full of faceless demons tried to ram and sink the golden boat. Before the attack reached its conclusion her parents walked in and turned the water and boats to stone. Dirty grey cemetery stone. Her mother dangled a baby over the table and when Sarah tried to grab it she fell across the stone, felt its coldness, and the stone turned to earth that opened like a mouth, and she began to fall into a blackness that might have been death. Her friends saved her by hauling her upwards into the light of a rising sun.

Perhaps it hadn't been a transmission after all, only a dream. It had come at night, she remembered, when she'd been dozing loose-minded after a marijuana omelette. Soon after she'd booked the flight to India because it seemed the right thing to do, and she had already stayed in Paris for longer than intended - weeks instead of days thanks to a left-handed poet she'd met in a café. It was his fault she'd started drinking again, and smoking dope and French cigarettes which next day made her throat feel like an unswept chimney. They'd had sex a few times too, nervously at first, and she had insisted he wore a condom. She didn't want any more babies stolen from her.

It had all been rather quaint until the star signal reminded her of the mission and those who wanted to stop her. When the poet first saw her scar she'd told him about the babies - or baby, she still couldn't decide - and he'd taken it calmly, like a weather report. When she'd told him about the mission and her enemies, his reaction was quite different. At first he had laughed, thinking it was a joke. When he realized it wasn't he had grown distant at the same time as she planned to put an even great distance between them.

Such were the vagaries of life, she thought, as a clutter of plastic trays switched her to a different wavelength. A stewardess handed her a meal she didn't want, something in her dark Air France eyes suggesting crumpled sheets and permissiveness. Sarah smiled at her. The woman's eyes flashed an acknowledgement, but her sexy mouth remained rigid. She reminded Sarah of a special girlfriend she once had: Susan, a lesbian whose company she had enjoyed, in an experimental sort of way.

2

THE CODEBREAKER AND THE LESBIAN

Sarah recalled the last time she had met Susan. It had been on the day everyone thought she'd gone mad. Had that been before or after the thing with the house and police? She couldn't remember, but knew for sure that it was the day it had all started - for other people. A day so vivid to her that it could have been yesterday, or even today.

She had made a soul-searing speech at school and shook everyone up with her insight and power. It had been a full-blown Christmas social during the last week of term, and she had been presented with an 'art award', a piece of paper covered with patronizing bullshit, handed to her by an old fart who didn't know Dali from Dallas. On that day her love of art had been stolen, for she had painted for herself, expressed her imagination in acrylic and oil for her own satisfaction. What did she care what others thought? Ever since the wretched idea of the presentation had been spawned she'd felt under pressure, under scrutiny, like a performing dog waiting for the lash of the cane when it drops the ball off its nose, trips over the hoop, craps in the ring. Her parents, of course, stressed how much they were looking forward to it, and of course other parents would be there, some their neighbours, an aspect her mother had found particularly appealing. As usual mother had eschewed physical contact - her tendency in general - and launched into a mixed bag of praise and concern underpinned with criticism and threat sprinkled with expectation. Her father had at least been straightforward and conveyed his pleasure with a hug and quiet words of praise.

After the uproar caused by the speech she'd been dragged

away by her stupefied parents and pushed into the car, in the back, like an embarrassing old relative, perhaps an aunt with no idea how to apply make-up. Then they had driven home, mother quacking at father - Janet and Bill, brunette and twill, threat and kill - her mouth disgorging words that sounded like meat cleavers in various stages of dismemberment.

And then a glance over her shoulder, eyes dark, full of menace, an intensity beyond words beaming out and filling the back seat like a heavy noxious gas.

Once home they'd called the family doctor, an ageing man known simply as Dr. Carson. Sarah met him with a sly smile in the lounge, after he'd had a lengthy chinwag with her parents. For a moment he had stared into her eyes, probably noting the size of her pupils, the intense green of her irises. Then mother had spoken, her voice a force that could travel years and lose none of its presence. Suddenly the past was the present, the aircraft a house in Oxshott.

"We've told Doctor Carson about this afternoon, and he'd like to talk to you about it."

"Yes, it sounds like you livened things up a bit."

"Introduced a certain awareness," Sarah confirmed, the irony unintentional.

"Your parents are understandably concerned about what happened."

"I know. They think I'm on drugs but you want to make sure." She looked decisively at her mother. "Don't you?"

"Your behaviour was out of character," Carson cut in quickly, "and is naturally a cause for concern."

"People don't like free-thinkers. They think they're a threat to their equilibrium. They tried to silence me and I exercised my rights by resisting them, but they overwhelmed me, like they always do."

"Who are they?"

Not a question she really fancied answering at the time. Her response had been a vacant examination of the carpet, as if they might have been lurking within it.

"Answer the doctor," her mother prompted.

Sarah looked up at her with a contemptuous scowl, then faced Carson.

"They are those who through their ignorance, fear and bigotry, their dirty prejudice, seek to oppress, repress, suppress, isolate and finally destroy either those elements within an individual that are different to what is desired, or the individual herself."

Carson licked his top lip. "Give me an example."

She didn't, and when the silence lengthened uncomfortably, her mother said, "Come on, Sarah, what do you mean?"

"Yes," chimed father. "It can't be difficult to think of one."

It wasn't, but it was difficult to divulge. "You," she finally whispered. "Both of you."

"What?" It was mother, her feathers ruffled. "That's ridiculous, Sarah. We've given you every opportunity - ."

" - and in return I'm a threat to their uniformity. Same with school, the teachers, all the bullshit on the television, in the papers, everywhere."

"That makes you sound like an outcast," Carson replied.

"Not really. I'm more like a rebel fighting a corrupted immune system."

"Acting alone, or with others?"

"Acting alone but under the guidance of others."

"And who are these others?"

Sarah smiled and didn't reply.

"I suppose a rebel has to keep some things secret. That's okay." He reached beside the sofa, pulled up his medical bag. "Would you mind if I gave you a quick check-up? Nothing complicated, just a superficial run-through to make sure everything is ticking along nicely."

"I don't mind."

Carson checked her eyes, pulse, heart and lungs, asked if

she had recently experienced headaches, unusual period pains, stomach upsets, visual disturbances, hearing problems, difficulties with eating or going to the toilet, insomnia, strange recurring thoughts, explosions of temper, lack of concentration.

She shook her head to every question, a permanent smile fixed on her face. Carson returned the smile frequently, like an uncle enjoying a private joke with a niece. Finally he announced that there appeared to be nothing physically wrong. However, he wanted to talk to her alone, and to keep the rules of confidentiality from being completely broken, suggested a walk in the garden.

"Talk about what?" Sarah asked, suddenly suspicious of his motives.

"Oh, this and that," and he turned to her parents for approval.

"It's getting dark," mother observed.

"I can put the garden lights on," father countered with a certain satisfaction. "The garden looks pretty when lit-up."

Sarah went to the downstairs cloakroom, put on a coat and a pair of chunky black shoes, then led Carson out through the kitchen and across a patio that stretched across the width of the house. Halfway up the garden she stopped, looked back, saw her parents silhouetted behind the sliding patio doors of the lounge. Shadow master and shadow mistress: she almost expected them to dance like puppets.

"Bit chilly," Carson said, buttoning up his sports jacket.

"Yes, it's December."

"You're an intelligent girl, Sarah, so I won't insult you by pussy-footing around. If you've got problems that are proving an unbearable strain, please tell me. I assure you it will be in complete confidence."

"As complete as asking me in front of my parents if I've been seeing things, hearing things, missing periods and shitting properly?"

Carson raised an eyebrow. "I don't believe I asked you those questions quite like that."

"The form doesn't alter the essence."

"I'm sorry if I upset you back in the house, but I had to ask you something while your parents were there, otherwise they'd think I wasn't doing my job properly."

Sarah scanned the garden. "Winter is such a contrast to summer. There's an emptiness about it, a hollowness of being, as if the spirit of the earth has fled."

Her words forced Carson to look around. The warm pools of coloured light that broke up the cold darkness gave him the impression of artificiality, like the landscaped gardens of a four-star hotel. Beyond the illuminated area stretched an arc of forbidding blackness.

"It must look beautiful in the summer," he said.

"Yes. The gardener does a good job considering how big it is."

"Do you have green fingers?"

She inspected her hands. "No."

Carson picked up on the unexpected tangent. "But you paint?"

"Sometimes."

"And write?"

"Sometimes."

"I was never much good at writing - you know what they say about doctors' handwriting."

"No."

"Always illegible. What do you write about?"

"Oh, this and that," she replied with a mischievous grin.

A breeze flicked hair across her face. She pulled it back behind her ear, heard a sigh, remarkably human. She turned, expecting to see a third person standing close, but there was no one.

"What's the matter?" Carson asked.

"Thought I heard something, but it was only the wind."

And the sigh came again, longer this time, and tinged with annoyance. She ignored it, not wishing to alarm the doctor.

"So, what's the problem that brings me here?" Carson asked, feeling that enough time had been spent circumventing the crux of the matter.

Sarah faced him squarely. "The problem would appear to be my parents thinking I have a problem."

"No problems at school? Bullying, unwelcome attention from teachers, pressure to perform to high standards, that sort of thing?"

"I go to a private school. We don't have those sort of problems."

"Really?"

"Yes, really. Bullying is less prevalent amongst girls, and if I were a victim of bullying I'd be less well liked by my peers, have inadequate social skills, lack confidence and self-esteem, and have suicidal tendencies. I think you'll agree that that doesn't sound like me, and if I thought a teacher had it in for me I'd complain about it. As for pressure, life's full of it. It's part of the deal."

Carson was almost impressed. "Do you do psychology at school?"

"I do social studies as an informal filler. We sometimes dip into psychology as one would expect. I think I've got a book or two on it."

Carson put his hands in his trouser pockets to warm them. "Why did you decide to make such a strong stand at the school today? To the point of upsetting your parents and others?"

"I felt I had to - and it's not my fault they were shocked. I can't be held responsible for the way people think and act. If they didn't like what I was saying they should have covered their ears or walked out. People like them make me sick. They're the ones who watch a TV programme then write in and complain about it instead of switching to a different channel or switching OFF!"

Carson flinched. "Emotive subject, eh?" he said awkwardly.

What was the silly old goat talking about? His grizzled grey beard and thinning ash hair? His zebra eyebrows and booze-ruddled nose, already blooming like a - .

"Red cauliflower," shrilled a voice.

She spun round, eyes searching the light and dark. "Did you say that?" she asked Carson.

"Say what?"

She looked up at the overcast sky. "No star juice tonight. Too much phlegm." She peered at Carson. "Do you believe in UFOs and alien life forms?"

"I keep an open mind. Do you?"

She looked thoughtful. "Sometimes my mind is too open." She stared into a cluster of coloured lamps that lit up a pond from beneath an evergreen shrub. "They remind me of multicoloured frog spawn emitting rainbows."

"Yes, they do a bit." They stared at each other for a moment. "You have a very active imagination, very vivid. What do you do when it becomes too much?"

"Use it more often."

Carson came nearer, his expression serious enough to hold a warning.

"Let's stop playing games, Sarah, and talk about your problem - and don't tell me you haven't got one. I've been a doctor for over twenty-five years and I know when people are lying to me."

"Really? That's a long time of deceit."

"Have you been taking drugs, Sarah?" he asked firmly.

"Sure. I take drugs every day. They're in the food I eat and the water I drink. They're in the air I breathe and in the clothes I wear."

"I mean street drugs. Cannabis, amphetamines, ecstasy, LSD."

"Sorry Doc, can't help you there."

"Okay Sarah, let's go back."

"You go back, have a chat with mum and dad. I'll stay out here, have a walkabout, inspect the estate."

"That's very considerate of you. Thank you."

She watched him stroll back to the house. Pathetic sod. So clumsy and stupid. Mother'll probably pour him a brandy to warm his ailing bones, then huddle with dad and hang on his every word, like the brainless followers of a bullshit guru.

She dampened her thoughts, moved into the darkness on one side of the garden. Flowerbeds beckoned seductively, blank rectangles of moist soil awaiting the touch of genius. She took off her shoes, her feet sockless, and walked heavily across them, forcing earth between her toes, against her ankles, sensing arousal in the minor freedom, an eroticism that tempted her to strip off, roll naked, rub mud into her skin until it was stained for ever with the Earth Mother's dark oil. Then fear of discovery made her panic and wipe her feet on the lawn. She put her shoes back on, tied the laces carefully. Looking across to the house she wondered what they were saying about her.

Before she could move the kitchen door opened, releasing an ingot of silver across the patio. A girl appeared, walked towards her. It was Susan, a friend from school.

"Hi Sarah. What are you doing out here? It's so cold."

"It's December and I'm looking for anything that doesn't fit."

"Like you," breathed a voice in her head.

Susan moved closer, touched her arm. "No kiss hello?"

Sarah looked her up and down: brown shoes, grey socks, black jeans and whatever was hidden beneath her older brother's black overcoat. The collar was turned up around her slender neck, her face pale, blond hair cut short.

Susan cocked her head to one side. "You okay, Sarah?"

"Yes, Sue, I'm okay," and she hugged her.

They kissed passionately.

"You're a dike," Sarah told her when they'd finished.

"You will be too, one day."

"I don't think so."

"I heard your speech this afternoon. You got a bit carried away - or should I say you got carried away," and she laughed. "Jeez Sarah, what were you on?"

"A stage."

"You know what I mean."

"Do I? Everyone assumes I know what they mean," and she looked across to the house, "but I'm not sure I do." Her parents had drawn the curtains in the lounge. It rekindled her curiosity. And made her feel like sex in the garden. She turned back to Susan, began to unbutton her overcoat.

"What are you doing?"

"Getting horny," and she kissed her neck.

"It's too cold and your parents are in." Susan pulled away, rebuttoned her coat. "Let's listen to some music in your bedroom," and she smiled suggestively by way of appeasement.

"Come on then, but be quiet when we're inside," she added. "I want to listen to what mum and dad are saying to the doctor."

"Doctor? What's he doing here?"

"They think I'm ill or taking drugs. Fucking morons." She caught Susan's look of surprise. "Really! Can you believe it?"

"And are you?"

"Don't be stupid."

In the kitchen they removed their shoes, Susan frowning at the dirt on Sarah's feet.

"They needed contact with Mother Earth. So did the rest of me but I didn't have the time." She put on her slippers. "Now don't forget to keep quiet."

"Perhaps it's not a good idea me being here, what with the doctor and everything."

"Are you my friend?" She regarded her hawkishly, suspecting treachery.

"Of course, but - ."

"But nothing," and Sarah kissed her on the cheek, crept out to the hall.

The lounge door was half-open. She listened intently while Susan stood leaning against a wall near the kitchen door, watching her carefully.

"Maybe she's got boyfriend troubles," she heard her father say.

Her mother replied, "She told me recently that she wasn't interested in boys, at least not for the time being. Probably just as well with her A-levels coming up. They'd only distract her."

Distract her. If only she knew the truth. Before she could turn and grin at Susan, the downstairs toilet flushed and Doctor Carson emerged. He said hello. She smiled at him, wondered if he'd washed his hands. Then Janet appeared from the lounge, all frowns and petty irritation as she glanced darkly at Susan then opened her mouth to speak.

Her only child swept in with, "Sue and I are going upstairs to listen to music. Is that okay?"

Her mother looked at Carson, who nodded.

"Yes, but keep the volume down."

Carson went into the lounge. Janet watched the girls go up the stairs. As soon as she heard the bedroom door close she went up to eavesdrop.

Susan stared around the bedroom as a shock wave engulfed over her.

"Jeez Sarah, what the hell have you done? It's crazy."

"I painted it."

"There's no doubting that. It looks like a paint bomb's exploded - you've even painted your computer - and the state of the place, I've never seen such a mess."

"Gets a drag being tidy. I did it last night or the night

before, I can't remember. My parents haven't seen it yet. Probably think the smell is just me doing another painting. They only come in now and again. I keep the door locked most of the time. Which reminds me."

She brushed past her to lock the door, dropped the key, bent to pick it up as the door swung open, hitting her head.

Mother stood in the doorway, face a scree of mounting horror.

"What the hell have you done?" she shouted, and with a sudden eruption of anger, "Just what the hell do you think you're playing at, for Christ's sake?"

"I've painted my fucking room, that's what I've done." Shouting now, fuelled by the pain in her head. "It's my room and I'll do what I fucking like with it and if you don't like it you can fuck off."

Dark eyes flared dangerously. A hand shot out, made contact, stung.

"Don't you ever talk to me like that - *ever*."

Head pain became cheek burn, triggered retaliation - a punch in mother's mouth.

"Like what?" Sarah screamed, "like what?" and as she went to hit her again, mother grabbed her arm and twisted it back.

They grappled fiercely, slipping on books and magazines, clothes entangling their feet, CD cases cracking under foot. Finally they crashed into the dressing table, scattering perfumes and make-up. Susan took the opportunity to bolt from the room, presumably meeting father and Carson before they rushed into the bedroom, the new colour scheme unnoticed as they pulled them apart. Sarah remembered struggling in her father's grip, screaming obscenities at her mother who stood shaking, from fright or rage she couldn't tell. Her father dragged her further back. Mother slumped on to a chest of drawers, blood trickling down her chin. Sarah continued ranting at her, driven by a skull-choir of discordant voices chanting *kill the cow - kill the cow - kill the cow - kill the cow -*

- and only then had her father looked around, his expression one of utter amazement.

The last sound she could remember hearing, once she stopped yelling, was Susan's car crunching gravel down the driveway. She never saw her again.

Sarah focused her attention on the food, the stewardess long gone. And now mother cow wants me dead. She jabbed her elbow inadvertently into the side of an adjacent passenger, an elderly plump woman of indeterminate origin. She snorted like a truffle-pig, glared malevolently at Sarah, who, sensing danger, turned to face the comfort of the window.

3

THE SHRUNKEN SHRINK

Alan Raddick sat in bed reading a book. Since his stay in prison he had developed insomnia, lost his friends, had his flat repossessed, been cast out of all the professional organizations he had belonged to, and joined the unemployed. He was broke, tired and depressed, with little fight left in him.

Prison had been interesting and horrible, and the same applied to the inmates and staff. They had taken great delight in teasing him, regarding him as a smart-arse psychiatrist with poor taste in women, who had not only been done over by the diminutive Melissa Burnham, but had failed to stay out of prison. But they didn't know he was innocent, and that Melissa was a nut smarter than himself. Now everyone regarded him as a criminal - had to be, he'd done time - and the pathetic maggot-like Melissa as a victim who had fought back, a heroine lauded by tabloid feminists. It was a rotten world, and since his release he had tried to claw his way back up, only to find every rung of the ladder broken by those he was trying to reach. At times he felt like a paranoid convinced that everyone was sabotaging his life at every opportunity. Hardly surprising: who wanted to be friends with a struck-off doctor who'd done time for attempted rape?

Melissa Burnham interfered with his reading. He put down the book, closed his eyes. She had a lot to answer for but he knew her actions would go unpunished. After his release he had tried to find her, out of curiosity or for revenge he still wasn't sure, but she had vanished and no one was inclined to help him track her down. Probably just as well, it would have been a time and money consuming task and although he had plenty of the former, he had precious little of the latter.

Luckily a light had appeared at the end of his impecunious tunnel. As he had been trying to figure out how to track down the girl who had ruined his life, someone else whose life had been turned upside down by the gentler sex was tracking him down. Bill Donaldson. Done over by his schizophrenic daughter and then done over by his psychopathic wife. Now the poor sod wanted him to find Sarah, assuming that he knew more about the inner workings of her mind than anyone else because he had been her consultant - at least until Melissa Burnham had popped up like a deadly new virus. Unfortunately he could no longer access Sarah's medical records, and as for her copious stories, essays, poetry and jottings that might provide a clue to her movements, they had gone up in smoke, or so the decidedly spiteful Janet Donaldson had said. And there was no way of checking because she had obtained a court injunction preventing Bill from entering the matrimonial house without first making an appointment with her, a condition she used as a further obstacle by making sure she was always out or too busy to see him. She'd changed all the locks, too.

Still, the loss of Sarah's outpourings was no big deal, because based on what Bill had read, and Sarah's main topics of conversation before she'd vanished, it seemed likely that India, or at least Western Asia, figured in her plans somewhere along the line. If not, tracking her down would be as hopeless as searching for an ant lost in space. Raddick laughed grimly. It was probably as hopeless as that, anyway. Nevertheless, Bill had already pumped money into an international firm of highly specialized tracers whose clients ranged from governments to millionaires with a chip on their shoulder. They had secured a watching brief on the passenger listings of every flight into Pakistan, India, Nepal and Bangladesh. Additionally they had checked lists back to the day Sarah had disappeared from her parents' Portuguese villa,

21

where Bill had taken her for a surprise holiday. The checks had drawn a blank, but the holiday had held more than one surprise for Bill. Not only had Sarah vanished, but she'd taken £20,000 in cash with her, money Bill had taken to Portugal in order to grease a deal he'd hoped to make. Sarah obviously had some ruthlessly lucid moments, a trait she may have inherited from her mother. She'd even left her father a note thanking him for the money, and explaining that it would finance the things she had to do. Unspecified things.

The European listings hadn't escaped the tracers, either, which is how Bill had found out that she'd flown from Faro to Frankfurt to Paris, where the trail went cold. Hardly surprising; she could have caught a bus to any number of countries, avoiding airports and with Europe's grand *ouvert* approach, not even being stopped at borders. Poor old Bill. Thought a holiday would do Sarah a world of good, and it probably had, but not the way he had expected it. Now he was desperate enough to spend astronomical amounts on finding her. Was that indicative of the depth of his love for her? Or was he guilty about something?

Ah hell, what did it matter what it signified? Certainly Sarah didn't seem to give a toss. She'd been incommunicado since Portugal. Smart move. Or was it? Maybe she hadn't planned it that way and it was just the way it had turned out. Maybe she was out of her head in a Brazilian prison, or wandering like a demented minstrel through the Kalahari Desert, or dead in Australia, a lucky mugger squandering her money on self-abusive activities. Searching for her without knowing her approximate whereabouts was an utterly useless exercise. Still, Bill was paying him a small retainer, a useful addition to his dole money.

Raddick resumed reading his book, an examination of Ki-Ching therapy, a new treatment that seemed to revolve around the maxim, 'Fuck the shrink, have a drink.' Five minutes later he hurled the book across the room and switched off the light, but Melissa Burnham drove sleep away with memories of their first encounter that were as fresh as the present.

She had turned up at his office late one morning, a studious type looking utterly plain and scrawny, with a posh reedy voice that bordered on painful. She'd written to ask if she could spend some time at the Kingston psychiatric unit where he had worked. She was doing a psychology degree and wanted a look at what went on behind the scenes. He'd written back suggesting a visit whenever it suited her. And that had been as good as the beginning of the end.

"I've heard that you have an innovative approach to mental ill-health," she'd said when asked why she had chosen him.

"Really? Where d'you hear that?"

"I heard it from two lecturers and three fellow-students."

Very precise, he'd thought at the time. Was she detail conscious? If so, was it part of a greater symptomatology indicative of obsessive-compulsive disorder?

"Did they tell you that many of my peers think I'm an arrogant maverick?"

"I must confess that I have heard such a slur."

Such a slur. Oh you nice person, Melissa.

He asked, "Do you think psychology is a true science?"

"Yes. Why, is that wrong?"

"Could be." And off he'd gone, the thoughts of Chairman Raddick - zap zap zap. "I often think it's a wobbly jelly made up of hard science, soft options, bad medicine, weak intuition, scrambled philosophy, hollow faddism, religiosity and ego trips. It wouldn't surprise me if the various contaminants in our lives are making us increasingly mentally dysfunctional. If so, then psychology could become an even greater breeding ground for mad one-eyed kings leading blind crazies into the grey mire of so-called experts' opinions.

"In the meantime we continue to develop as an increasingly self-damaging id-dominated world sucking in addictive pleasures - I want it all and I want it now! Money, food, drink, drugs, sex, violence, mind trips. Physical satisfaction. Mental captivation. Spiritual evisceration. The lure of the adrenalin high, the feeding of the habit, access twenty-four hours a day to whatever we want. And we must rush, because our time is precious. But precious for what?"

Melissa wasn't supposed to answer the question, but she was so eager to please, so eager to impress. "Perhaps our time is precious precisely because it is our time, to do with as we please," she'd said.

Lame, he'd thought, and she knew it. He reined in, gave her a chance to talk.

"Is it my tendency to step outside the confines of the medically orientated biological approach that interests you?"

"Yes. I understand that you are a rarity in the field of psychiatry because of your willingness to embrace other approaches - not the psychological model approach, because that's closely allied to your mainstay, the medical approach, but others such as behavioural, psychoanalytical and cognitive, even family, social and humanistic. I gained the impression that you feel all approaches hold some relevance in the investigation and treatment of mental illness."

Little did she know that he had never embraced other approaches, but had merely dipped in and taken what he thought was necessary, depending on the patient and the illness. He'd been a scavenger, a scrap dealer, and now others saw him as a loose cannon - thanks to her.

"Some people don't like the way I interact with my patients," he had told her. "They think I'm too hard on them. What they don't seem to realize is that some patients play games and need a firm hand, a kick up the arse."

Melissa had frowned at that, and delivered an unexpected broadside. "So do you concur with John Rosen and his direct analysis therapy, in which the patient is deemed to have a strong enough ego to handle aggressive verbal confrontation as long as it is within the parameters of a supportive relationship?"

He had looked very thoughtful before answering that question, simply because he hadn't been able to immediately remember who the hell John Rosen was. His answer had been a good one, though. "I think you'll find his approach was focused more on schizophrenia than anything else - talking of which I've a patient to interview. Her name is Sarah and she was admitted last night. You can sit in on it if you like, assuming she agrees."

Melissa's dull brown eyes had brightened a fraction. "Yes, thank you; I'd like that."

When Sarah arrived Melissa had stood, introduced herself, and held out her hand. Sarah sat down on the chair furthest from her, ignored her hand, and stared with undisguised hostility.

"Melissa is studying psychology and wants some direct experience of how we do things here, so I was wondering if you'd agree to her sitting in on our interview."

Sarah had watched Melissa take a notepad and pen from her bag, then looked at him and said, 'No - fucking - way.'

Sarah's answer hadn't surprised him. In her position he'd have refused, too. What had surprised him was the intense venom in the three words.

He had shrugged at Melissa and said, "I'll buzz reception and have someone show you around instead. Perhaps afterwards you could mingle with the patients in the lounge, talk to them, get the feel of the place."

"Yes, that would be helpful, thank you."

When she was leaving the office she had said, "I'll see you later - Alan." In retrospect her tone had been inviting and full of intimate promise, as though they were lovers. She'd smiled at Sarah, too, but her eyes had held a dark warning, as though Sarah might be a love rival.

After Melissa had closed the door Sarah had stared at it for a full two minutes before saying, "I don't like her. She's an impostor. I can feel it."

"What is she then?"

"A lying little bitch."

"Apart from that?"

"Dangerous."

And how right Sarah had been, for a month later, as her mother sat in his office for a progress report, the wretched Melissa Burnham had entered without knocking, and had stood in the doorway like a frozen caricature of womankind, her hand outstretched, holding a small box wrapped in pink and white bells and tied with thin crimson ribbon. She seemed shocked to find another woman in his office.

"I'm sorry, Alan, I didn't realize you had a patient with you."

"I don't," he'd corrected abruptly. "This is the mother of a patient and we are rather busy."

"I understand," she said moving forward. "I just wanted to give you this and wish you happy Christmas. Are you going to be at the party here tomorrow? The in-patients are looking so forward to it." She placed the box on his desk with a smile and moved back.

"No," Raddick lied. "Can't make it. Other commitments I'm afraid."

Melissa's smile drained off, her eyes narrowing a fraction.

"Well I shall be here," she informed him, "doing my bit." She glanced disdainfully at Janet, reached the door and said, "Maybe I'll see you later for a Christmas drink, Alan, or is that going to be another promise you can't keep?" And black lightning jagged across her face as she left the office and closed the door.

Raddick had grinned, and not wishing Janet to gain the wrong impression, said, "She's been hanging around here on and off since Sarah was admitted, ostensibly to gain insight through hands-on experience - she's a student doing a psychology degree. Unfortunately she's proving a bit of an odd nuisance. Keeps pestering me, trying to get me to have a drink with her."

"Seems like a variation on student-tutor infatuation. Perhaps you should make yourself look less like a younger version of Robert Redford."

Raddick caught a swift saucy smile that briefly lit up Janet's eyes.

"Is he a favourite actor of yours?"

"No. I was just giving you the benefit of a female observer's perspective. Of course, you could simply tell her she can't come here anymore, or make a complaint to wherever she's studying?"

"I think I will after Christmas." He put Melissa's present in a drawer. "Where were we?"

Better questions sprung to mind later, but had nothing to do with Sarah or her mother. His Christmas present had been a £500 Rolex watch which he didn't need or like, and despite not having seen Melissa for a month after Christmas, anonymous telephone calls came in waves every other day, the caller - it had to be her: who else could it be? - as silent as himself, and perhaps experimenting, too. To his mind Melissa Burnham was a disturbed young lady. Beneath her public superficiality he had glimpsed free-floating anxiety, obsessive-compulsive traits, narcissism, paranoia, and social unease - at least when interacting with the mentally well. Circumstantial evidence suggested her actions towards him were triggered by a strong and probably perverse fantasy life focused on desired, and in reality mostly unobtainable, relationships. A consequence of this was her smouldering hostility towards those she perceived as a threat to the development of her relationship with him. She was quite possibly borderline personality disordered, rather like the character portrayed by Glenn Close in the film Fatal Attraction.

How right he had been.

As the weeks rolled by the phone calls began to drive him nuts, but the silence had finally produced a result, and Melissa Burnham had spoken - angrily; hurt by his snubs, his lack of gratitude for the Christmas present, his lack of interest in her. He had told her he was flattered but that she wasn't his sort, and as wonderful as the present was, he didn't need another watch and perhaps she could take it back and get a refund, give the money to charity, buy some text books.

She had screamed at his suggestions.

"I bought that watch as a token of my appreciation for allowing me to visit, not to entice you into bed you conceited bastard. And I don't need the money from a refund - I've plenty of money and I don't need your self-serving charity. All I want is for you to wear it - and I'll know if you're not, and if you don't wear it then you'll really be rubbing salt in my wounds. God, Alan, your attitude is so disappointing. It really saddens me to have to talk to you like this. All I want is for us to be friends, have a drink occasionally, for me to be able to appreciate what you are doing in the field of psychology."

"Psychiatry," he corrected.

"Correcting trivial mistakes is one of your negative traits, Alan. You should learn to relax more and harmonize yourself to others, be more willing to overlook their errors. All I'm asking is that you treat me with respect, and in return you'll find I'm not half as bad as you think. In fact you'll find me twice as good. You'll see, Alan, really you will - but don't think I'm pressurizing you into this. All I ask is that you wear the watch."

"And if I don't?"

"You'll have a big problem. Goodbye Alan. I'll see you soon."

He had immediately telephoned the University of London to make a complaint about her, only to discover they had no record of a student with her name. When he had dug out her initial letter of enquiry, he found there was no telephone number to go with her home address in Putney.

He had stuffed the letter in his pocket, intending to visit the address when time permitted, to see what it was like. Then again, why bother? She was obviously unhinged to some degree, the sort it was best to steer clear of. If she did make life difficult he could tell one of his police contacts, see if an informal visit was possible to scare her off.

It was then that he had replaced his wristwatch with the Rolex, in case she did turn up unexpectedly. Why the hell had he done that? Had he been that fearful? He had also telephoned reception and instructed them to tell Melissa, should she visit, that he was attending to duties elsewhere. If the unit had a proper security team he would have instructed them to prevent her from entering the building.

Another thought had occurred to him then. Did she know what car he drove, its colour and registration number? Knowing her sort he surmised that she probably did, having already watched him from afar. If so, and she saw his old Volvo in the car park, then she'd know reception were lying to her - and if she had a car of her own, had she followed him home? The last thing he wanted was her creating a scene at his flat in Richmond. But if she had seen where he lived, she wouldn't know which flat it was, because the buzzers carried no names - unless she had asked a resident going in or coming out. The block was small, and run by a residents committee; everyone knew everyone else. The only consolation was that he had an entryphone to keep her out the building, unless she buzzed another flat under a different pretext.

Raddick's final thought on Melissa Burnham that day was that he could try and treat her, get to the root of her problem, help her out. It was something he knew she'd either react to negatively, or embrace only to be near him. It seemed he could do nothing but wait and see what she did next.

A fortnight passed during which he'd grown used to the Rolex but not to Melissa's inactivity. She was up to something, he felt sure, and he wanted to know what, so he could be ready for it, sort out the problem once and for all - before the daisy chain of hairline cracks hiding hurricanes on the periphery of his life shattered it completely.

He never had a chance.

She broke into his flat and smashed it up, but not before changing her address so the police couldn't find her. For a while it seemed she had vanished into thin air, but nothing ever really does. A few months later she had turned up at his flat one night, begging to see him. She desperately needed his help and was on the point of suicide. Against his better judgement he'd let her in, and once she'd calmed down she began talking about depression, giving little away about herself. In order to create a relaxed atmosphere and facilitate her self-disclosure he offered to make her a cup of tea. She had accepted his offer and it was then that everything had turned pear-shaped. As he had turned his back to go into the kitchen she'd hit him over the head with something and knocked him out. When he regained consciousness the police were banging on his door. They had found Melissa wandering half-naked outside the building, in a state of shock. She had told them he'd tried to rape her.

The police had taken him away and forensics had moved into his flat. Their investigations had uncovered evidence, for Melissa had been busy while he had lain unconscious on the floor. She'd taken his limp hands and scratched her arms and stomach with his nails, ensuring her skin tissue could be found beneath a few of them. She'd even added pubic hairs, and placed a few threads from her clothes on his. Then there was the bite mark on his hand, cuts on his shin where she'd kicked him in her fictitious defence, her solitary shoe in the hall, her torn clothes.

Despite his truthful version of events and his lawyer's protests, he had been refused bail and hauled off to prison, his profession, contacts and standing in the community as meaningless as truth itself. Naturally he had been suspended from his professional duties pending the outcome of the matter. And naturally Melissa smashing up his flat had been cast aside, a minor theory with no supporting evidence. For all her sins she had suffered no more than being a bogus voluntary in-patient at Charing Cross Hospital, a victim of crime in need of counselling. What she had really needed was a full-blown psychiatric assessment to prove she was deeply disturbed, but that had been pie-in-the-sky.

Raddick's hopes had rested with the court case, with witnesses from work stating how Melissa had been pestering him and displaying behaviour suggestive of a disturbed personality. But no one had testified on his behalf. Most probably believed he had done it, the police holding him because they had good evidence confirming guilt. A few of his fellow professionals had no doubt seen it as an opportunity to get rid of an irritating colleague. Even his notions to prove her evidence false had come to nothing more than the twitterings of an indignant fool who'd been caught.

The only consolation was that he hadn't received a longer sentence - and that had all been down to Melissa citing his previous good character and work in the community, and asking the judge for a light sentence to reflect these factors and prevent a basically good and intelligent man from wasting away in prison because his passions had overwhelmed him. And she had glanced at him then, and fucking smiled.

Raddick's reaction had almost got the better of him. A meltdown of pure hatred sucked in every perception and threatened to explode across the courtroom. How he had contained it he still didn't know, but it must have been evident in his face.

The judge had given him four years, but with remand time and good behaviour knocked off, he'd done two-thirds of that. Jesus Christ, it all seemed so bloody unbelievable.

Yet she was still out there - or he assumed she was - and if she was, what was she doing? Did she know he'd been released? Was she still obsessed with him? He recalled how she had twisted everything to her advantage in court, played a performance worthy of a dozen Oscars. The woman was dangerous, worse than a virus. If she surfaced again, what would it cost him? He shook his head, suddenly depressed in a dark, angry sort of way.

4

MUMMY KILLER COW

Janet Donaldson sat coiled on a sofa in the matrimonial home, a sizeable four-bedroom detached house in Oxshott, Surrey. It was stockbroker green belt with publishing executives like her, and advertising directors like absent Bill. The stockbrokers had moved elsewhere to nurture their fledgling moustaches, nurse their penis extensions, and get pissed on barrage balloon salaries. Many seemed to roost at Canary Wharf and other ugly perches in Docklands - or Poxlands as Janet preferred to think of it, remembering an arrogant shit who not only couldn't fuck any better than a turtle, but had given her NSU into the bargain. In return she'd given his precious Ferrari a brake fluid shampoo.

She looked slowly around the large lounge. Like the rest of the house it seemed suddenly small and ordinary, and far too suburban. Occasional redecorating and refurnishing because of Sarah's destructive antics had not only cost them dear, but had eroded whatever creativity the place had originally held. When her plans reached their rightful conclusion she would sell the house and buy a huge apartment overlooking one of London's parks, and in keeping with her natural inclinations, entertain more suitable men in the style she thought they deserved, which historically had rarely been in the style they thought they deserved. There was nothing quite like taking a man who might prove useful in the future, coaxing him with or without intoxicants into a bit of hotel bondage play, then using him cruelly until he was begging for her to stop and untie him so he could go home and lick his wounds. By which time she'd usually taken a few exceedingly embarrassing photographs of the fool and mailed them to a post office box number in the West End, from where she transferred them to a safety deposit box in a nearby bank. The tactic was used sparingly, and the relationships rarely lasted longer than the initial night. Not many men got off on sadism when they were the victims. Her collection was nevertheless interesting.

The NSU turtle had been a mistake when she was younger, an office party fling that had left her seething for days after. But she had learned valuable lessons from the experience: target selection and justification, psychological styles of seduction, and giving as little as possible of herself. Shrinks into Freud would draw her father into every encounter, but she wasn't concerned about the veracity of that belief. To her it was simply another way to accumulate power, a callous strategy of which, together with her childhood abuse, Bill remained ignorant.

Bill. What to do about him. He was rapidly becoming the non-sexual pox of her life, but one that had to be maintained before treatment to terminate. There was no doubt in her mind that he was up to something. There were the frequent telephone calls asking if she had heard from Sarah, his easy agreement to her demands regarding the divorce, his pleas to visit the house on the pretext of discussing things with her, his evasiveness when she asked him what he was doing and where he was living, and the anxious calls from the Armstrongs in Epsom about Bill sitting in his car near their house, probably hoping for a glimpse of his grandson.

Grandson! More like the bastard offspring of the demented.

Three weeks after leaving Raddick's clinic, Sarah had met an old boyfriend while shopping in Leatherhead. They'd gone back to his place, smoked dope, listened to music. Made love - probably fucked like animals - and then Sarah had gone home happy. But parents were always the last to know, or so it seemed. Two months later Sarah reduced the maintenance dose of her anti-psychotic medication. She hadn't liked the way chlorpromazine occasionally made her mouth dry, or gave her a stuffy nose, made her legs feel weak, or blurred her vision; made her feel she was always suffering from something or other. And no one suspected the real reason.

It came on Sarah's eighteenth birthday, during dinner at a pretentious French restaurant. It came during a lull in the conversation. It came mid-chew. Without preamble.

Janet remembered freezing in mid-movement, staring at Sarah like a stranger who'd just been insulted. Bill had frowned hawkishly at his plate, as if an earthworm had emerged suddenly from one of his snail shells. Janet had felt tension and a draining of blood. Then Bill had looked up and blinked like a barn owl.

Sarah had looked expectantly from one to the other, a gleam of enjoyment adding intensity to the green of her eyes. Bill had let out a sigh. Janet wiped her mouth with a napkin.

"Are you absolutely sure?" Janet had asked, in a tone that had broken the silence like ice cracking under pressure.

"Oh yes. There's no doubt whatsoever. The father is a biker in Leatherhead but he doesn't know about it, and I'm not going to tell him, because he's been in hospital, too, for manic depression, so he has enough to deal with. A baby's not what he needs in his life right now."

Janet's eyes had almost popped out of her head. "You're keeping it?"

"Of course. Why not?"

Why not? Why not?

A row followed and Sarah had walked out. Next day she had left home, hidden herself in Acton, West London. Janet shook her head. The place was fit for the spawn of the mad. Horrible. But they had eventually found her, too late to abort, but with time to plan post-natally.

The birth had been a straightforward Caesarean section, necessary due to Sarah's mounting confusion during labour and lack of cervical dilation. The baby was a healthy boy and Sarah never saw him. He was suckled by surrogate tits and 'adopted' soon after birth by Roger and Judith Armstrong, a wealthy couple cursed with double infertility. They named the boy Eric, an unimaginative name but one that she thought perfectly epitomized the Armstrongs and their precious Epsom suburbia.

The whole escapade had cost Janet six thousand pounds, blood money to which Bill had refused to contribute. His involvement, however, cost his conscience more, and that was something to smile about.

Janet pictured the Armstrongs cooing over a pram, fingering the baby's face. Given half a chance Bill would be doing the same. The images made her feel sick. More so when she reflected on Sarah's arrival into her world.

She had clawed the walls, her antenatal expectations a horrible delusion, the responsibilities of motherhood a burden she despised. She had been a career woman happy in the cut and thrust of business: looking after a baby was irksome, unfulfilling, a waste of her potential. She had no mothering instincts, no sense of bonding, no love. The baby was simply a bloody nuisance she wished she'd never had, a thief who'd stolen her career and independence and replaced them with mindless servitude in an upmarket prison surrounded by an acre of land, her warders a twice-weekly cleaning lady and a gardener who patrolled the grounds with a wheelbarrow.

Her resentment had intensified unceasingly. She blamed Sarah for everything: waking, crying, feeding and shitting; missed opportunities and her own isolation; and Bill's long absences on business trips - any excuse to get away while she acted the role of loyal housewife and mother. And ultimately it had all been his fault for persuading her how lovely it would be to have a child, and filling her head with romantic nonsense.

As the situation continued without respite, she seethed. In

the presence of others she had acted out a false adoration. Alone with Sarah her animosity had grown, and with it a dangerous darkening of her personality, until one sleepless night she'd held a pillow six inches from Sarah's face, almost overwhelmed by a desire to smother her. A memory surfaced then, from so deep down it almost smelt of sulphur from the vents at the bottom of her past. Clinging to it like an exotic translucent form of mnemonic life was a feeling close to inverse déjà-vu: "Don't struggle my little angel, or the pillow will cover your face and block out the light and air, and it'll feel like you're being buried alive." Her long-fingered father. And he had done it.......once, and it had felt like being buried alive, or at least how she had imagined it as a child.

The memory and feeling had brought her to a stop - would she have stopped without them? - not only because she had been close to smothering her own child, but because he had done it to her, and so now father and daughter, separated by life, death and relentless time, shared part of a common action, albeit with different motives. The fact was repellent.

Realizing that she was fast approaching the point of no return, and not wishing to admit her shortcomings to anyone other than herself, she had decided to make a few changes in her life. Without consulting Bill she had secured an executive position with a publishing company, fired the cleaning lady and employed a nanny - none of which had surprised Bill, or so he had said at the time. The only surprise was that she had held out for so long - did that mean he could see she was having difficulty with full-time motherhood? If so, why hadn't he said something, done something? Or did he want her to self-destruct because he was having an affair? She recalled him saying how he hoped the new job would make her happier, improve their own relationship, and remove any subtly pernicious influences from Sarah's life. Subtly pernicious influences? So he knew something hadn't been right, yet he'd done nothing to help her or Sarah. And then he'd prattled on about her already being more like her old self, and after congratulating her on the job he opened a bottle of champagne to celebrate. Before he'd even finished the first glass he was asking about the nanny. Typical. Sex at any opportunity, with people like her left to bear the consequences. Just like her father when he wanted sex and would dote over his only child in preparation, while his wife - Janet couldn't think of the woman as her mother - sat in another room lost in alcoholic depression. But sex to father was planting poisonous kisses all over her body and jerking off. Once the bastard had come all over her and left her to clean it up, his affection ended and he became as cold and distant as everything else had been back then. She was lucky it had happened no more than eight or nine times and he hadn't progressed to penetrative sex. That may have been far harder to cope with. She may have gone the way of his wife and killed herself. Or him. As it was he died soon after she had escaped to university. A cerebral haemorrhage, not exactly the sort of punishment she would have liked, but at least it removed him from the planet.

Increasing anger forced Janet to cut short her reminiscencing. Now the bloody Armstrongs were panicking. Was Bill having second thoughts? What if he spills the beans? Why is he upsetting us like this? Every time one of us goes out to speak to him, invite him in even, he drives away. He's outside every week. The neighbours are beginning to notice. What have we got to do - move?

Janet had felt like screaming at them: *Yes, move, go to fucking China and stay there!* Instead she had reassured them that it was all psychological. Bill was just coming to terms with the situation, assuaging delayed guilt that would soon pass, and when he drove off quickly whenever they appeared, it was because he was too embarrassed to face them. It was nothing to worry about. But Janet knew it was, because when she asked him about it he had denied being anywhere near

Epsom, never mind outside the Armstrong house. It was then she had called in a top-notch detective agency. Now Bill couldn't fart on the phone without her knowing about it.

The agency reports had so far been unsettling. Bill was trying to be too clever by half. He'd been meeting Alan Raddick, now out of prison. Exactly why wasn't known, but Sarah seemed a safe enough guess; she was the only thing they had in common. Perhaps she'd surfaced and they were planning something.

As for his suspiciously easy agreement to the terms of the divorce, she now knew he had considerable assets world-wide that she hadn't previously known about. Money stashed in secret bank accounts in Switzerland, Austria, the Cayman and British Virgin Islands. Properties all over the globe. Bulging shares in the best blue-chip companies. And other investments that by themselves made her divorce settlement look like a casual handout to charity. If he thought she could be fobbed off with the house and a few hundred thousand pounds, then he was sadly mistaken.

The icing on the cake were his visits to the Armstrong house: they suggested kidnap. If it wasn't for her own involvement in the baby's adoption, she would have been only too happy to secretly and indirectly help Bill kidnap it - and get caught doing it. Thankfully, because of the overall circumstances, there was a far better alternative.

The evidence suggested Bill wanted to find Sarah, reunite her with her son, with the three of them retreating to a sunny clime where they could all live happily ever after - but not before she was hosed down and left to rot in penury.

The divorce settlement was a ruse to remove her from the scene as quickly as possible. The strategy showed how naive Bill could be. He was operating subjectively rather than objectively, and she would show him to what extent that was a mistake. But not yet. A few more details on his hidden assets and then she would be ready for action - with a vengeance.

If Sarah wasn't found soon, she would withdraw her acceptance of the divorce settlement on the grounds that Bill was withholding information on his financial status and those assets she had a right to claim on. If necessary she would threaten him with court action; the worry would weaken him. At this stage in the war winning all wasn't the main point; chipping away at his confidence and playing for time was.

As for Raddick, she already had him under surveillance, and surprise surprise so did someone else. The agency's men had taken photographs, maintained a tangential surveillance, and had quickly found out who the newcomer was. When she had seen the pictures and read the report, her delight had been so great she took the rest of the day off and went shopping in Harrods.

The person was no other than Melissa Burnham, living in a room in a West Hounslow lodging house, no form of employment evident. To use this deranged groupie in her plans was tempting, but for the moment the idea was on the back burner pending further developments. If Raddick became a nuisance, Melissa would find herself with an unexpected ally, unless she went loopy in the meantime.

On the other hand, if Sarah was discovered overseas or returned to England of her own volition, then her plans would have to take on a new dimension. Using the darker contacts her detective agency maintained, the easiest option would be to arrange a little accident. Perhaps a large dose of LSD. It was known to push some on the cusp of schizophrenia into the real thing, so it stood to reason that someone already with the illness would end up further submerged in madness, hopefully to the point of requiring life-long treatment as a permanent patient in a residential psychiatric institution. If that happened there would be no point in Raddick and Melissa hanging around, and Bill's options regarding kidnapping and reunion would be redundant. She could then focus on getting her share of his money and making her own happy ending at his expense.

However, there existed The Far Better Alternative.

She had a mole in Bill's solicitor's office, and knew he hadn't changed his will, and if he was kept busy wouldn't do so for a while. As it stood, his assets were to be split fifty-fifty between herself and Sarah in the event of his death, and if Sarah was medically certified as being incapable and incurable, then she might be able to manoeuvre that share, minus fees for the loony-bin, into her sphere of jurisdiction or better still, into her possession. But the real juice in this plum plan was that if, perchance, Sarah died too, she'd get the lot without any legal hassle, and wouldn't be lumbered with the fees, either. Yes, she felt like a hanging judge with the power of life and death.

Unfortunately the whole thing could go down the tubes if Bill decided to change his will prematurely. If there was so much as an atom of a hint that he was going to do it, she'd have to bite her tongue, swallow her pride, lay on the charm, perhaps even make overtures about a reconciliation. Tell him the balance of her mind had been disturbed by Sarah's illness and work pressures, but that she was better now and realized the underhand adoption of Sarah's son had been wrong and what could they do about it, how could they make it up to their daughter? Oh, she felt so guilty, felt as if she were emerging from a nightmare. How can I make up for all the terrible things I've said and done, Bill? How can I make things better?

Come round for dinner, a few drinks, a little.......murder. She laughed. Maybe she'd let the fool have her. It had been a while since she'd been put through her paces, and it would give him the chance to recreate what had been, at first, an enjoyable part of their past. Lure him in, play for time. No murder until she had his full balance sheet before her and knew what goodies were available. Then she'd get rid of him. But if he didn't take the bait and give her the time she needed?

Or Sarah reappeared and screwed things up? Expediency over greed. She'd just have to bring things forward and settle for less.

The base line wasn't whether she had the moral deprivation to arrange the murders - morals didn't come into it - nor if she could, if necessary, commit them herself. The base line was her own survival: the safeguarding of her assets and the potential to increase them, the security of her power base and its future expansion. In short, the money. At least two million pounds she knew about, and much more she could only guess at.

5

INDIA

After a brief stop in Karachi, Sarah disembarked in Delhi, leaving the aircraft to continue to Bangkok and beyond. The airport wasn't as bad as she had anticipated, probably because it was six in the morning. She walked nonchalantly through customs, the officials apparently more interested in stopping prosperous Indians than bothering with her - until suddenly one of them crossed her path and without slowing said with a tight half-smile, "Vulcan say it okay."

Sarah stopped abruptly, watched the man disappear through a doorway. Had she heard him correctly, or had he been mumbling to himself in Hindi and she had misinterpreted it? As another official stared curiously at her, she felt a hot flush of panic and hurried to a bank counter, changed some money and made for the exit, securing a seat on a battered old bus destined for Connaught Place, the centre of Delhi.

Sitting by a grimy window at the rear, she mulled over the airport incident. Wasn't Vulcan a Roman god or planet or something? As the bus ground into gear and shuddered off, she came to the conclusion that she had misheard the official. Happy with that explanation, she settled back to enjoy the ride and her first glimpses of this new and mysterious land.

Her first glimpses became a ten minute feature as the bus stopped after a few minutes and the driver disappeared into a wooden shack. Bored, Sarah slipped away with the driver and explored another mysterious land, one which was oddly familiar yet dreamily unfathomable.

The stepping stones into young adulthood had been fused from the grindings of confused emotions. Teenage ignorance had replaced childhood innocence, and clashed with the strictures of adults and their clumsy attempts at guidance: the subtle but constant pressure to perform well at school, do her homework, pass exams, act cute in front of her parents' friends, like an exhibit whose achievements gave mum and dad something extra to boast about.

As adult influence fluctuated in importance, the counterforce of her opinionated and less sophisticated friends increased. With the careful pacing of dawn, she had realized that her conscientious ideals would have no place in what she perceived as the cynical, corrupt and hypocritical reality of future adulthood. Either she changed or dropped out, it looked that simple.

She had soon found out that it wasn't, and had grown increasingly preoccupied with whether or not she could do either. The more she thought about it the more she questioned who she was - her parents' dream child brimming with intelligence and full of startling potential? A puppet who couldn't reach the standards set by others unless she allowed them to pull her strings? Or a person destined to carve out a niche in a totally unexpected and creative way?

Every question she had asked herself spawned another, and every day had brought different answers. The lack of clarity became a source of painful perplexity, and she'd felt like a rebel who hadn't yet found a cause. Worse still, she harboured the suspicion that despite the vast choice of causes on offer, she would never find one worth embracing.

To her mind environmental causes had come too late in the day to make much difference, and humanitarian causes, because of their constantly recurring nature, had made her wonder why anyone bothered. Others, such as political causes, had left her cold. It seemed all of them suffered from a lack of direct sustainable action, as if a perverse etiquette dictated that only symptoms could be treated while underlying reasons had to be left intact to ensure the future continuity of effect and action - the cause's justification for making a business out of itself - like treating gangrene with pain-killers instead of cutting it out, thus ensuring profits for the drug giants and everyone else caught in the web of their own making.

Everything back then seemed to suck, and ultimately, as the future unfolded countless times in her mind's eye, the images had polarized and she saw that it could be easy if she acquiesced to her parents wishes, or hard if she exercised defiance and chose the up-hill struggle for self-determination.

When she had sought advice from her father, he had replied like a mathematician describing an obscure equation, and said that if she wanted she could work for him once she'd passed her A-levels and the degree. Her mother, out of earshot from Bill, had responded with a flurry of words that summed up her personal philosophy for success: pass the exams, build up the right connections, marry into money, work hard, be ruthless and climb fast. And never settle for anything less than the best from those around you.

The answers had come across as the equivalent of a creative strait-jacket, and had served only to emphasize her father's staid protectionism, her mother's cold ambitions, and her own isolation. She had desperately wanted them to understand her confusion, her struggle to forge a compromise between the forces of life and her own inchoate feelings.

A third choice had been to turn her back on the familiar and embrace the unknown, travel the world, perhaps doing odd jobs along the way until she arrived somewhere to which she felt a mysterious affinity - a sense of belonging - and settled. Whatever way she had looked at it, life had seemed either comfortable and shallow or problematically profound, with an escape route between the two.

And now the escape route had led worklessly but madly into an Indian bus parked outside a shack by a field on a deserted road.

Her fellow passengers - seven of them - waited without complaint. When the driver eventually appeared without an explanation, he turned the engine and gunned the bus down the road with a screech from the gearbox.

The bus cut across flat fields speckled with squatting men openly defecating, entered featureless city outskirts where little groups sat brewing tea round fires and makeshift stoves, then passed the colonial houses of the Chanakyapuri embassy district before terminating at the end of Parliament Street in the inner circle of Connaught Place.

The area was virtually deserted and Sarah was struck by its space and cleanliness. She sat on a low wall, pulled out a map of Delhi covered in notes she had made from a traveller's guide to India. She wanted the Ringo Guest House - it reminded her of Ringo Starr - in Scindia House, which she assumed was on Scindia Road, a fair walk from her position. As she looked around for a three-wheel auto-rickshaw, she noticed a Sikh with pointed features standing by her shoulder. The discovery of his presence gave her a nasty turn and she jumped to her feet, bag clutched close to her chest.

"What do you want?" she asked him curtly.

The Sikh moved his head in a peculiar fashion, neither a nod or a shake, and his eyes struck her as rather intense.

"What's wrong with your head? Have you got a loose fitting?"

"Yes," he eventually replied. He rubbed his nose, hawked up phlegm, spat it out behind the wall. "Rickshaw?" he said.

"Tuk-tuk?" she asked.

He frowned. "Took-took?"

"If that's the way you say it - yes. Do you know the Ringo Guest House in Scindia House?"

He moved closer, pointed to a black and yellow tuk-tuk parked a short distance away. She hadn't noticed it before and when she looked around she saw a few more. She repeated the question.

Yes," he replied.

"How much?"

"Twenty."

Probably a rip-off, but after more than fourteen hours of travelling she couldn't be bothered haggling over the fare. She walked with him to the tuk-tuk, climbed in, bag on her lap, the map open on top of it. The Sikh turned the engine, which sounded suspiciously like a lawn-mower, and did a left turn to follow the inner circle of Connaught Place.

After completing a quarter of the circle he turned left up a stony side street then swung right into a narrower road. Buildings closed in and acrimonious smells forced their way up Sarah's nose. Every minute or so the Sikh, hunched in his seat, turned and smirked at her, revealing hints of treachery. His dark eyes held a sadistic edge; his pointed nose reminded her of hawk-like Arab bandits; a neat black beard suggested a wicked Asian corsair with a curved sword and cruel crew. Had any of the demons on the black boats in the restaurant had a face, it would have been his.

The road grew rougher, the tuk-tuk swinging wildly round potholes, missing the odd dog or human by mere millimetres. They crossed two main roads, traffic and people increasing in stages, giving the impression of a long trip. As they raced up a muddy alley, old and musty with piles of rotting garbage, buildings met above them, casting them in gloom. Sarah squinted at her map and wondered where the hell she was being taken.

No sooner had she thought that, then the Sikh shot her an angry glance as if he had sensed her doubt, and that for her to suspect any ulterior motive on his part was adding insult to injury. She wondered if he could read her mind, insert his thoughts into hers, extract her own and destroy them. She grew increasingly uneasy as they sped on, the speed and wild manoeuvres suggesting great desperation, as if the Sikh was racing against time itself.

His backward glances became furtive glimpses in the ill-positioned rear-view mirror. His eyes narrowed to slits through which Sarah saw a calculating brain growing more and more frenzied as the odds lengthened and time ran out. She felt a sudden rush of adrenalin as panic flashed through her like a bolt of lightning.

Travellers' cheques, cash, passport, duty-free cigarettes - yes, he wanted them all, she knew, the thieving dacoit, and this was how it was done. The shifty, cheating - but perhaps he was just heading for the right road? No. It felt as if they had almost completed an erratic circuit of Connaught Place; and besides, too many pedestrians were staring at them in that knowing way, as though aware that the tuk-tuk ride was the last journey she would ever make.

Choice, she thought, that the forsayers of her doom were Indian strangers she'd never seen before, while those closest to her were thousands of miles away - weren't they? - and totally oblivious to her rapidly approaching demise. It showed that those closest to her had never cared enough to be attuned to the signs, and that these dark strangers had the sensitivity to perceive what wasn't obvious. Damn! Damn them all - friends, strangers and the whole poxy world. And just as she was getting her mind straightened out, too. What an irony! An ignominious end in Delhi, robbed and murdered in some dirty alley smelling of piss and cow shit. And on her first day here! Fuck fuck fuck and she didn't even have a knife with her.

The tuk-tuk rejoined the original curving road, swung up Jan Path and stopped with a shudder outside a shabby building. Sarah peered out. No way was this grubby little street full of stones Scindia Road. She looked at the building. It was Scindia House.

"Ringo," breathed the Sikh, pointing at a large corroded sign.

Sure enough it was. With a flush of relief Sarah paid him and climbed up a narrow flight of stairs to a small reception area at the top. A lean young man behind the desk said the hotel was full. A nervous tremor in his voice made her think he was lying. He recommended the neighbouring Sunny Guest House. A false smile and eyes betraying an inner anxiety made her doubt his recommendation. Maybe he was in league with the Sikh - or God forbid, her mother. Or Jesus Christ her father too, hunting for his money. She quashed her paranoia and went next door to have a look.

A pleasant bushy youth with a good command of English offered her a single room with attached bathroom for the equivalent of three pounds. She asked to see it. From a cursory glance it appeared reasonable enough, so she took it. After filling in the hotel register she collapsed on the bed. It was eighty-thirty. Within minutes she was asleep.

6

THE MONEY BUCKET MAN

Bill paid Raddick a dawn visit. It took five minutes of bell-pushing before he appeared in a dressing gown, two days stubble on his face.

"Sorry to wake you so early, Alan, but it's urgent."

Raddick hid his surprise and invited him in.

"I apologise in advance for the state of the place. It's pretty grotty."

"I know, I've been here before."

"Yes, of course you have. I'd forgotten. Must be still half-asleep." Raddick led him up a dark flight of stairs and into his bedsit. "Am I right in thinking Sarah's been found?"

"Yes. I got a call from my agency a couple of hours ago. She landed in Delhi around midnight our time."

Raddick's tiredness left him as his interest shifted up a notch. With luck his retainer might become a decent fee for something proactive. Bill wasn't keeping him close out of friendship.

"Is she under surveillance?"

"Yes."

"What's she doing?"

"Nothing. She booked into a cheap hotel used by backpackers, and hasn't left her room since arriving. I think she's probably sleeping."

"Did they say anything about her appearance and behaviour?"

"I asked, and apparently she looks okay, just like any other young foreigner arriving in India. They didn't notice any odd behaviour."

"What do you want me to do?" Raddick was beginning to feel a twinge of disappointment, a suspicion that his services would be dispensed with now the professional bounty hunters had found her.

"Come to India with me. You know Sarah's inner workings better than me - or Janet. Do you have any immediate plans?"

Raddick smiled without meaning to. "Only an interview for a crappy job. How long do you think we'll be away?"

"Hopefully no more than a week."

"Then count me in." He gestured to a shabby armchair. "Sit down. Do you want a cup of tea?"

Bill sat down, refused the offer of tea, and looked around. The walls and ceiling were nicotine white. The three piece suite was a hideous red and orange tartan. Wrinkled prints of anonymous countryside covered one wall. A small dark table and two chairs stood by windows overlooking the street, their net curtains grey. The television was an antique. Dust covered everything.

"What happened to your flat when you were in prison?"

"Repossessed. I had a silly notion that I could pay the mortgage from my savings but it didn't work out. I lost it, and everything else. Even my father doesn't talk to me now."

"What about your mother?"

"Died when I was fifteen. I've got a brother living in the States, and a sister in Glasgow. We don't keep in touch. Would you mind if I went and put on some trousers?"

"Don't worry about that for now, I don't have a lot of time this morning," and he came straight to the point. "Okay, this is the deal. I'm prepared to pay all the expenses and give you five thousand pounds before we go, and the same again when we get back with Sarah. The arrangements will be done through one of my companies; you will be a consultant under an open-ended contract."

Raddick was sure his heart had stopped beating. "Sounds like manna from heaven. What about the men out there?

Won't my presence annoy them?"

"Sarah is just a small part of their daily workload, and as you're a psychiatrist your presence can be regarded as a medical necessity, so there shouldn't be any bad feeling. Okay?"

"Ex-psychiatrist, Bill. I was struck off - remember?"

"Who in India is going to know that?"

"Yeah, you're right." He ran his fingers through his hair, combing it back. "What do we do when we get there?"

"Get her out and back here using any means necessary."

Raddick did his best to look like an old friend. "Sarah's illness can make her very unpredictable, Bill."

"I know. We'll take it as it comes."

"If she has a relapse out there it may complicate things. We can hardly drug her and carry her on the plane like hand luggage."

"I know that, too. Contingency plans exist. I'll even charter a private jet if it comes to it."

Raddick detected a touch of ruthlessness and impatience in Bill's manner that he hadn't noticed before. It intrigued him. And there was something else he couldn't put his finger on.

"When do we go?"

"Tonight."

"Tonight?"

"Yes. Is that a problem?"

"Life's like a coral reef. It takes years to put together and only a few seconds to rip apart. I'm unemployed and friendless, living in a grotty Isleworth bedsit paid for by Hounslow Council, and what's left of my possessions are in storage. I'm still angry over what happened and now I've got depression looking over my shoulder. How can it be a problem?"

"I sympathize with your predicament, Alan, and I hope that together we can alleviate it."

"Thanks Bill, and I'm sorry, I didn't mean to come across

as a whinging has-been." He forced a smile. "What about our visas and jabs?"

"The visas can be done this morning through one of my contacts. You'll have to get some photos done and give me your passport - have you got a current one?" Raddick nodded. "The jabs won't make any difference at this late stage. You'll just have to make sure you're careful when you're out there."

"If I get typhoid I'll expect a bonus."

"Private health care at the very least."

Raddick's expression turned serious. "I hope you don't mind me saying this, Bill, but I get the feeling there's more to this plan of yours than meets the eye. Something that adds an urgency over and above what is required."

Bill's face turned hawkish for a moment, unhappy with Raddick's insight. "There is," he said, the words dissolving his reticence. "Janet's been exercising her muscles and playing clever. I found out yesterday that she's been using a top detective agency to keep tabs on me."

"Because of the divorce?"

"Partly."

That he had overseas assets of more than four million pounds was none of Raddick's business, but Janet was certainly trying to make it hers. How she'd found out about their existence he didn't know for sure, but her agency hacking into computers or greasing palms would be a fair bet. They had a reputation as good as the one he was using. Whatever their methods, if she succeeded in locating his assets her divorce settlement would increase dramatically, and she'd no doubt make sure the Inland Revenue took an interest in what was left. As for the Epsom affair, he didn't want to think about it.

"What's the rest of the reason?" Raddick prompted.

"I think she hopes to find Sarah through me."

"Why?"

"I don't know. She's made it clear that once the divorce

goes through Sarah is to be my responsibility, which is fine by me."

Raddick sensed danger. Janet reminded him of Melissa Burnham. Mad and cunning.

"Have you seen or spoken to her recently?"

"I've seen her once, briefly, when I caught her leaving work, and we've spoken several times over the phone."

"What's her state of mind these days?"

"She came across as very haughty when I saw her. Over the phone she's been obstructive."

"More stroppy than normal?"

"Yes."

Raddick detected resistance. "And?"

Bill pursed his lips, unsure if he should tell him more. Finally he decided to come clean, see if Raddick's knowledge could throw light on Janet's mind and motives.

"She's become much darker, more paranoid and vindictive. She's always had a slightly warped streak in her nature, and during the last year or so it's got worse. She's become more power hungry and selfish. To tell you the truth, before we separated I often wondered if she was a little unbalanced in some way. Nothing too obvious, just a sinister sort of detachment, especially when dealing with anything of an emotional nature. A lot of the time I'm sure she put on an act for the sake of outsiders, but in the home it was as if the act wasn't good enough and I could see through it."

"This was before or after the onset of Sarah's illness?"

"Both, but more noticeable after. In fact, when I look back I can see many instances when her emotions seemed genuine but were probably false. Sometimes living with her was like living with a time bomb waiting to go off. She likes to get her own way, always has, and the more she gets it the more she wants it. Does any of this make sense?"

"Yes."

Bill waited, then said, "So what do you think, having met

54

her numerous times when treating Sarah?"

Well, thought Raddick, it's not only pimps, conmen, murderers and drug dealers that can qualify as psychopaths or sociopaths or whatever you want to call the condition supposedly held by five percent of the population. Is that the same five percent that emerge as leaders in their chosen field? There are plenty of business executives, politicians, salespeople, doctors, builders and bar staff that also qualify. Yes, Bill, your wife is probably an incurable psychopath, one of those inhabiting the upper echelons of the classification. Superficial charm and above average intelligence; considerable poise, calmness and verbal ability; egocentricity with a splash of *ouvert* narcissism; poverty of deep and lasting emotions; untruthfulness and insincerity; lack of remorse; a lust for power, manipulation and money - she's got them all.

"Is the question that difficult?" Bill prompted with sudden impatience.

"Sorry Bill, I was just thinking back to the times that I'd met her. Obviously I can't determine if she has a problem without a proper psychological assessment, but in view of the circumstances what you've said suggests we should be careful."

Bill inhaled rather too sharply, obviously dissatisfied. "I appreciate that, but I was hoping for a little more substance. Especially anything that can be connected with why she wants to find Sarah."

"That's an even harder question for me to answer, especially as we don't know for sure that she wants to find her. It's pure speculation at the moment. Maybe she just wants to know what you're doing, and if you find Sarah, what happens to her. She may still be concerned about her welfare even if she doesn't want to be actively involved with it in the future. On the other hand maybe she wants to use Sarah as a pawn for leverage in the divorce."

"Can't see how Sarah would make any difference."

"What if Janet assumed responsibility for Sarah as part of the divorce settlement, insisted on a large sum of money being set aside for Sarah's future treatment and well-being, which she would control with the intention of using for her own purposes?"

"Any such money would be in the form of a special trust fund approved by a court and administered by a lawyer. Janet wouldn't get a penny except for reasonable expenses backed by receipts which could be checked."

"So Sarah would make no significant difference to the size of the divorce settlement?"

"Correct." What was a couple of hundred thousand when millions were at stake?

"So why so much interest in Sarah? I feel we need to broaden our horizons." Raddick's train of thought headed into darker territory. "Have you made a will?"

"Yes, I did one years ago."

"I don't wish to pry into your financial affairs, but who are the beneficiaries?"

"Everything is to be split fifty-fifty between Janet and Sarah - which reminds me, when we get back from India I'll have to do a new will, and change a life insurance policy that names Janet as the beneficiary."

"Wouldn't it be better if you did that before we went to India? We don't know what might happen out there."

"That sounds sinister. What are you expecting, my death?"

"Of course not. I'm just being cautious."

"Uhm, well, in answer to your question, a new will is not something I can jot down on a piece of paper and have witnessed by whoever's around. My affairs are far too complicated for that. Accountants and solicitors would have to advise me on a number of things before I could make a decision about who gets what."

Raddick straightened up as a nagging theory pushed out from the darkness.

"This may sound crazy, but what if Janet wants not only what she'll get from the divorce, but everything else you've got - except Sarah."

"You've lost me."

Raddick wondered if he really had. Now he was going to have to spell it out.

"As it stands now, if you and Sarah die Janet gets everything, and as a bonus she is rid of a husband she is getting divorced from anyway, and a daughter she doesn't much care for."

Bill was so shocked it took him a while to find his voice. "Are you suggesting that Janet could be thinking of having Sarah and myself murdered?"

Now Bill had said it, the suggestion seemed extreme, even ridiculous. "It was just a thought," Raddick said with a shrug.

"And a wild one at that. Janet playing the she-devil is one thing, but murder? Of her husband and daughter? No, I can't believe that."

"I know it's unlikely, but all possibilities should be considered. After all, we have absolutely no idea what she's thinking."

"I'd like to know exactly what you're thinking about Janet."

Raddick pursed his lips, gathered his thoughts, and told him the truth.

Bill appeared to visibly deflate. Janet being a psychopath was something that he hadn't considered, but then before the family doctor's informal diagnosis he hadn't thought of Sarah as schizophrenic. The shortfalls made him feel ignorant, blind to what seemed so obvious to others. He felt vulnerable again, as vulnerable and powerless as when he had first heard Dr. Carson explaining Sarah's illness.

"It has nothing to do with a split personality as many people think. That's a different illness called multiple personality disorder. With schizophrenia the personality fragments. This is because it's primarily a thought disorder, with emotional disturbances forming a secondary symptom level.

"What happens is that thoughts and emotions become disconnected from each other, and tend to function separately and incorrectly, producing inappropriate behaviour and delusions. The delusions often replace or overlap large chunks of reality, and although some untreated patients appear to function reasonably well at times, most have difficulty recognizing the difference between reality and fantasy, and their behaviour obviously reflects this.

"Another prominent symptom is hallucinations, mainly auditory rather than visual - voices in the head, voices coming from domestic appliances, that sort of thing. Incoherent speech is also common, because of the thought disturbances, and this extends to the written word.

"Most schizophrenics don't even realize they have a problem."

Janet had asked, "How does it differ from the split personality - multiple personalities? Because that's what it sounds like to me."

"Imagine a circle with a horizontal line through the middle. In the top half you have thoughts, in the bottom half you have emotions. The line represents the split disconnecting the two halves. With multiple personality disorder the line is vertically positioned, creating two different personalities, each having its own thoughts and emotions which function normally together to form the basis of the personality. There could be several such vertical lines, and indeed a few people have been known to have more than fifteen personalities. Incidentally, the disorder is usually the result of the patient having been abused as a child, who during the period of abuse forms satellite personalities within which to live. A form of inner escape that ultimately becomes a prison. Quite a different beginning from that which concerns us."

"What causes schizophrenia?" Bill had asked.

"No one knows for sure, but it is believed to result from the interaction of at least two things: a genetic propensity and on-going stress or sudden trauma. Drugs like LSD, marijuana and amphetamines can exacerbate development of the condition, and to a lesser degree, alcohol. Other possibles include neurotransmitter defects in the brain - too many or too few transmitters or receptors, or a defect in the passage of signals between them or in the signals themselves, or even a combination of these things. Obviously such defects could have a genetic basis, although it's possible they might be caused by other factors during life. Nothing's been conclusively proven one way or the other. Other reasons which have been suggested include vitamin and mineral deficiencies, diet, and the inability to properly digest certain foods, resulting in a build-up of toxins produced by intestinal bacteria getting into the blood stream and affecting the chemical balance of the brain. My personal belief is that the cause is a combination of factors."

"Is it curable?" Janet had asked.

"The prognosis is good if treatment is maintained. In Sarah's case we may be able to nip it in the bud, but you will both have to be supportive - and watchful. It's easy for schizophrenics to forget their medication and have a relapse."

"How long does treatment last?"

"A few months to a year. Sometimes longer."

"How much longer?"

"Years."

"How many years?"

"Until they die."

Carson became Raddick and Bill regarded him with sudden suspicion, as though he might be wrong, or joking, or not really there at all. But he was there, with a grim expression and a hint of sadness in his eyes.

"Sorry, Bill, but you did insist."

"I know, and a question has just occurred to me. If Janet is a psychopath, shouldn't she be receiving treatment?"

"Psychopathic disorder is regarded by many as untreatable. Besides, in Janet's case, what is there to treat? It's like personality disorders, they only come to the attention of the mental health services when particular personality traits get so exaggerated the person can no longer behave normally at home or work or socially. For example, everyone can get a bit paranoid to some extent, and it can be a useful survival tool in society and business. But if it becomes unjustifiably exaggerated and twisted to the point where a person can't go outside for fear of, say, being assassinated by government agents, then treatment would be needed. Psychopaths don't usually come to the attention of the health services until they've committed a crime. Most don't, of course. They just go through life doing their thing, like the rest of us."

Bill deflated a little more, nodded a tired understanding. "Thank you for being so frank. I think I'll have that cup of tea now. Then perhaps before I go to work we can find a photo-booth for your visa photos."

"Sure. I'll put the kettle on and get dressed."

7

KALEIDOSCOPE

A loud bang woke Sarah. Metal striking metal somewhere outside. Her eyes opened to a musty yellow greyness. Pale light streamed through the window into one half of the room. The door came into focus.

She sat up, looked across to a chest of drawers expecting to see her bag on it. It wasn't there. What a fool! She'd forgotten to lock the door and some shifty bastards had made off with it. As she leapt from the bed she saw the bag on the floor, snatched it up and checked that the bulk of her father's money she'd stolen from Portugal was still in it, then checked that the rest was in the money belt beneath her loose fitting top. Satisfied all was well, she took an antipsychotic chlorpromazine tablet from a bottle of one hundred provided by a pharmacist she'd fucked in Paris just before she'd left, then lit a cigarette and pulled the curtains further back.

In the dusty yellow light the room showed up as basically clean and tatty, with mottled cream walls, an inconveniently located mirror, orange linoleum, a green door and a grey ceiling from which hung a rickety brown fan. The air smelt of old dust and damp clothes. She flicked the switch to operate the fan. It turned in a hesitant manner, as though cutting effortlessly through the air was beyond its capabilities. It made her think of a pterodactyl that amazed by staying airborne.

She stepped into the windowless bathroom, switched on the light. It wasn't much bigger than an upright coffin with a western-style toilet and sink, a shower head directly over the small space between them. The cistern top was missing and water trickled over the edge and wound its way down to a drain, which also marked the termination point for a plastic hose originating from under the sink. Cholera and typhoid flashed into her mind - did I have the jabs? - and memories of syringes and pain drove them away. It was the sort of bathroom she didn't want to touch with even a finger nail; however, she had no choice and the toilet worked, ending the overflow and creating a new trickle that filled the cistern.

Sarah washed, changed her panties and top, sat on the bed smoking and studying her map of Delhi. It was three in the afternoon. Where could she go? The main bazaar, Pahar Ganj, wasn't too far away, and she decided to take a leisurely stroll in that direction. The main sightseeing - Red and Old Forts, mosques and temples - could wait another day or two.

She double-checked her money belt, left the room, closed the door, then remembered the rest of the money. As she went back inside a misshapen shadow with spiked arms and a twisted body vanished from over the bag. She stood rigid, her mind struggling to make sense of the little she'd glimpsed. Had it been a trick of the light? A fleeting shadow cast by something outside, a cloud or bird passing in front of the sun? Or an hallucination? None were very convincing, and with a deep breath she walked further in, looked in the bag, remembered that she'd already checked it, and after a final look around locked the door, hoping that whatever she'd seen wouldn't be waiting for her when she returned.

Inconsequential things took on a new dimension in the subcontinent, and Sarah's face soon fixed into a permanent smile as she soaked in everything, revelling in the new sensations like a child, awed and stimulated almost to the point of being overwhelmed.

As she moved north away from the modernity and ease of New Delhi she encountered sporadic shanty dwellings of wood, plastic, corrugated tin and cardboard, many erected within the gaze of glass and concrete office blocks. The bright clothes of the slum dwellers contrasted soberly with their depressing conditions, epitomised not only by their hovels but also their daily chores such as washing utensils or children in roadside gullies of murky water.

Initially it was the incongruities of her new surroundings that struck Sarah with most force: a prematurely aged woman, sari collected up beneath her as she squatted over a task by the roadside, staring enviously at a pretty high-caste girl wearing make-up and a fashionable western outfit; an ox and cart from distant rural pastures holding up the progress of a sleek limousine; a skeletal beggar twisted in rags outside a shop selling videos and satellite dishes; pyramids of dusty fruit on dirty blankets alongside Delhi's answer to McDonald's; the smell of urine and exhaust fumes mingling with the aroma of cooking and sweet spices - the whole a kaleidoscope of sensory input, an arcane heaping of dissimilars.

Soon the outskirts of the dustier, more crowded Pahar Ganj beckoned, its dense maze of native delights luring Sarah into its teeming interior.

She wandered along several streets crowded with shops, stalls and pavement hawkers selling sacks of spices, nuts, rice and dal; stainless steel cooking pots, carpets, silks and gems; foodstuffs, raw cotton, old engine parts and tools; wood and marblework and dubious antiques; shoes, clothes, medicaments and bhang. Occasionally a merchant would shout out an invitation for her to enter his shop, or she would be accosted by an ear cleaner, head masseur, astrologer or chiromancer, or a dealer in secondhand spectacles or false teeth, even scrap paper and dirty rags, the quest for business untiring and essential.

As with the merchandise, so with the smells: cinnamon and cumin, fruits and farts, sandalwood and sweat, perfumes and piss, rotting vegetables and a hundred more too subtle or fleeting to guess at, and within this rich tapestry were woven horns, bells and whistles; yells and laughter and creaking carts; the clip of hoof and the patter of feet; the music of words and the music of souls; the ripples and waves of life.

Occasionally Sarah loitered and watched the people: farmers, peasants, schoolkids, beggars, cops, young men in jeans, turbaned warriors, barefoot hags, and beautiful young girls in bright saris, their ankles and wrists adorned with silver chains and glinting bracelets, baskets of produce sometimes balanced on their heads, hair partings crimson, foreheads dotted red, their hands often tattooed with strange symbols.

India had Sarah in its clutches, and that afternoon she would have willingly spent the rest of her life there. It was a universe away from Oxshott, London, Portugal and Paris.

She ambled along, bewitched, until a pale shape appeared before her, causing her to stop. A grinning brown face materialized above a white shirt and fawn trousers. The man peered into her face.

"You have the most beautiful eyes I have ever seen," he said. "They are emeralds from the gods, to be treasured and loved."

"Fuck off," Sarah replied as she brushed past him, angry that his crude overture had contaminated what had so far been a wonderful afternoon.

As he came alongside her, she stopped and glared at him.

"Please please, I did not mean to upset you. I was only paying you a compliment. It is not often I see such beautiful eyes filled with so much untamed mystery that they compel me to stare into them so rudely."

"Are you hoping to hypnotize me?"

"I do not have the skill, otherwise I would be a most wealthy man." Sarah found that funny and laughed. The man continued. "Are you by any chance interested in meditation or yoga, or what is in the stars?"

"Uhm, maybe the stars. Why? Do they talk to you?"

"Come, I will show you. It is not far. You can partake in

some chay and discuss your stars more fully. Knowledge of the future is always worth knowing."

For a moment Sarah was sealed in a noiseless, timeless cocoon, totally unaware of her surroundings. Her brain tumbled out ill-formed scenarios at a rapid rate. Was this an elaborate form of kidnap or robbery, some crazy Indian scam where she'd end up in chains getting raped by every man in the city? Was he crazy and talking trash, perhaps a schizophrenic like her? Or was he telling the truth? He looked harmless enough, and she felt sure she could sort him out if he tried anything unpleasant.

"You might put poison in my tea," she said.

The man tutted, looked hurt, but a smile forced its way through and he said, "You do not have to drink tea if you do not wish to. Only listen and talk, and you can leave when you like. It is for you to decide how important your future is. I think your stars will reveal much of interest."

"Are you a salesman?"

"A salesman?" He looked hurt again. "It is a lowly employment best suited to those who have nothing of their own worth selling. I do. I have the key to the gateway of knowledge. Come, let me show you."

"Don't you advertise in the papers?"

"I'm sorry, I don't understand."

"If you had something of your own worth selling, you wouldn't need to bother strangers on the street."

"I do not bother strangers on the street. I merely alert them to something of importance which would otherwise pass them by. Like their future. Your future." His gaze intensified. "What it holds for you."

Sarah was quick. "If it didn't hold anything for me it wouldn't be my future, would it?" She wondered if he knew anything about Vulcan or the star signal, or what her parents were up to. "I have received messages from a star called Vulcan. I am on a mission. Do you know anything about this?"

The man stiffened, spoke earnestly. "This is important. I can find out more for you. What is your mission?"

Sarah had to think about that. "Uhmm, it's personal, you know?"

"Yes yes, a very important consideration. We should go now, and see what we can discover about it."

The pressure was on again and she didn't know what to do. The offer was tempting, but if he was lying? She needed to know more about him.

"Where did you learn enough English to switchblade your way through a conversation? You sound too clever to me. What's your game?"

The man wondered what switchblade meant, and said, "I was taught English at school, and have studied it since. It is very important in India. It helps those who talk different languages to talk to each other, otherwise no one will know what anyone else is saying." He paused as Sarah nodded her understanding. "I also play no game. Games are for merchants and those who have nothing or everything. I only wish to provide you with enlightenment." He glanced at his wristwatch. "Time is moving on, and soon the opportunity will be gone for I have much to do today." He cocked his head to one side and raised his eyebrows.

"You're not part of some religious movement, are you? A recruiter for Hare Krishna or that Bhagwan lot?"

The man failed to hide his exasperation. "No no no. I am just an ordinary fellow wishing to help you with your secret mission."

Sarah rubbed her chin and stared at him. There was only one way to resolve this encounter without leaving a mystery, and that was to go with him. Satisfied he wasn't likely to be a murderer, slave trader or rapist - his face was too soft and his frame too thin and he was shorter than her - she finally nodded her assent.

They weaved along the street, Sarah behind him, and turned into a narrow road. Halfway down it tapered into an alley that twisted like a sick worm between tall dirty tenements. Not once did the man turn to see if she followed, and she found that odd. Odder still was the fact that he hadn't spoken to her since they'd set off, as though doing his best to ignore her. Suspicious once again of his real motives, she let the distance between them lengthen and toyed with the idea of running off.

Suddenly he stopped at a big brown door and banged a large brass knocker. The sound reverberated down towards her and shot something cold up her spine. She glanced behind and froze. Dozens of blank faces with hostile eyes peered at her from windows, doorways and the alley walls. They stared with the silent grimness born of deprivation, stared at the stranger in a strange land, their land, and through that brown door - they knew.

The man looked at her. "They are poor people, uneducated but curious. They do not see many foreigners coming to this house."

And leaving it? Sarah thought of the official she'd overheard at the airport. Had he been warning her about this? Was he, in fact, the man?

A bolt shot back harshly and made her jump. The door creaked open revealing an impenetrable blackness. She followed the man inside, smelt strawberry incense. The door creaked shut behind her. She turned as the bolt grated back into place, saw an ill-defined shape, lighter or darker within the blackness she wasn't sure. As it took form she detected a faint sweet scent, heard the rustle of fabric, knew it was a woman.

The woman moved across to a thin band of ground-level light and opened another heavy door. Sunlight flooded across flagstones, illuminated the blue, green and gold of a sari before revealing the woman to be a young girl whose beauty was beyond words. Sarah stood transfixed until the man touched her elbow and broke the spell.

The girl led them into a large tiled inner courtyard in which stood plants in earthenware pots and a pond with a disused fountain. Divans draped with soft rugs encircled the orange-dappled water. On one sat an old man attired in something resembling light brown pyjamas and an embroided dressing gown. His head supported a white turban and his feet were hidden in a pair of soft black slippers. He was feeding goldfish with crumbs and stood as they approached him.

The girl veered off; the two men talked in low tones; Sarah stood self-consciously, annoyed that she was being ignored. The conversation ended with laughter, her guide walking off into one of the many rooms surrounding the courtyard. Sarah wondered if they had been laughing at her. The notion fuelled her paranoia and she stared none too kindly at the man with the turban.

"My apologies," he said with a slight bow. "Please excuse my manners. I am not used to having such an attractive guest in my humble abode. Please sit down," and he indicated his divan.

Sarah sat at the opposite end from where he'd been sitting, and looked him up and down. His height, agility and style of dress belied his years. His face was sparsely lined but what lines there were ran deep. His eyes danced with a life of their own, green-flecked hazel in pure white, knowledgeable and virtuous and due to their colour, not very Indian. The mouth turned up at the corners, below it a trim black beard. His fingers were long with manicured nails. Sarah guessed he was a man who had gone through life with ease and humour. And as she cast her eyes over him so he cast his eyes over her, then took up his original position on the divan and clapped his hands.

The girl reappeared with a silver tray of steaming tea. Sarah guessed her age as fourteen or fifteen. A small gold ring in her nose made her decide to get her own pierced before she left Delhi. Silver rings on her fingers and toes, and mysterious red tattooes on her hands and arms, sent her down other avenues of thought. When the girl leaned forward for Sarah to take her tea, sunlight lit up one side of her face and the smooth hairless skin glowed golden brown.

For a second their eyes locked, as if something of significance was to pass between them. Nothing did, and when the girl moved back her large innocent eyes seemed to hold a vague desire. Sarah wondered what it would be like to taste her delicate lips, unravel the sleek raven hair that hung platted to her waist, kiss her slender neck, suck her silvery blue finger nails, her silvery green toe nails, and let slip the elaborate majesty of her sari. When she felt a twinge of passion between her legs she blocked off the thoughts and watched the girl leave the courtyard, movements as graceful as a butterfly, the sun dancing on her silver earrings and bangles.

She had never seen such beauty. The girl was undeniably exotic, erotic - and somehow robotic.

"Real, and yet unreal," her host said quietly. "She has no vocal cords, and if not for the soft rustle of her sari she would move with the same silence."

His voice emphasized the sudden otherworldly peace in the courtyard, something ethereal and pleasant that permeated Sarah's mind and calmed it, and in doing so, relaxed her body.

"Who is she?" she whispered.

"A goddess.....like you." He looked curiously at her. "I can feel it."

Sarah tensed. "I only came to have my stars read. Your friend brought me here." She looked around as if he might reappear. "Who was he? I thought he was going to do it. I didn't expect all this elaboration."

The man sipped his tea, put down the cup by the pond, and adjusted his position as if preparing to deliver a lengthy monologue.

"Please allow me to explain. My name is Azad; I am an astrologer, palmist and psychic. The man who brought you here is Ravi, an employee. I am very successful with a prestigious clientele, and therefore I have no need to send employees out to look for more clients. However, on rare occasions a person with a particularly unusual aura is encountered and invited back to see me. If Ravi misled you then I once again offer my sincere apologies."

Sarah grappled to make sense of it all. Finally she said, "What's so unusual about me? I'm just a traveller."

"You are giving out very strong signals. Already I can feel them without the need to touch you, or look at your palm, or draw up your birth chart. This in itself is unusual."

Bullshit or what? Sarah couldn't decide. She needed to hear more.

"So what are you feeling?"

Azad launched into his usual routine. "You have an inner strength which is quite remarkable, and a sense of purpose in your travels which is.......intriguing. I feel as if you are being led somewhere. Something strong is drawing you in, like a magnet. But it is more. It is psychic, telepathic.......almost spiritual. It has bridged the gap between itself and you, and the bridge grows stronger with each day. Even now I can feel it, and it is very powerful."

"What is it?"

Azad closed his eyes, jerked slightly as words came unbidden into his mind. "It is something primitive," he blurted. "Ancient. Pure. It is pushing you to the east." He opened his eyes, trying hard not to reveal his confusion. When he saw Sarah staring attentively at him, he looked down at his hands. They were trembling.

"Is it Vulcan, the star signal?"

Azad closed his eyes again. Ravi had tipped him off about Vulcan and the possibility that she was a little crazy, perhaps

70

a druggie. Most of the foreigners who took him seriously and paid him well were one or the other, or desperately searching for a spiritual anchor-point, and those who weren't came simply out of curiosity and still paid him. On rare occasions he did experience genuine insights, and spoke the truth, assuming that those who heard it had been destined to hear it from him, and those he bluffed hadn't. It was as simple as that, and business was business, and no one went away totally empty-handed. Even lies and his hastily concocted astrological charts held a grain of truth. As for this girl beside him, anything vague and ambiguous would serve to fire her imagination, give her something to grasp and enlarge upon. The only problem was that nothing was going to plan.

"It is the heart of a child," he informed her, his words surprising him. "Yes, definitely a child." By all the gods what was happening? He had never before come across such powerful psychic manifestations - and of all the times for it to happen, it had to be now, when he least wanted it.

"Are you married?" he found himself asking her.

"No."

"You have a brother or sister?"

"No."

"Perhaps a son or daughter?"

"I have a baby. I'm looking for it. It was stolen from me."

Azad tensed. Was this why they wanted to capture her? Because she was making life difficult for someone? He didn't want to know. His role was simply to give her the tea, go through his normal routine while she drank it, and when she passed out let others take her away. A simple enough job for the amount they were paying him. Except he now sensed a darkness that suggested danger of a different kind closing around her.

"You must be very careful."

"Why? Are my parents after me?"

"I don't know, but I can sense great danger - not here now,

but elsewhere, very soon."

"In the east, like you said earlier?"

"Yes, but I don't know where. The warning signs I am receiving are blotting out everything else." He opened his eyes in alarm. "Whatever have you done?"

"Nothing," Sarah replied indignantly.

"You haven't drank your tea. It will get cold."

"It is cold."

He leaned forward to take her cup. "Let me get you another."

"No thanks. It's got cinnamon in it."

"I will get you tea with no spices."

An urgency in his voice and manner alerted her. "No thank you," she replied firmly, placing the cup on the floor. "I'm not thirsty."

"But you must. It is the custom here in India when one is a guest."

Sarah's response was loud. "I don't want any tea - okay?"

Azad sat back, held his hands up in a placatory gesture. "I am sorry. Please excuse my manners." If she stormed out she'd take the plan with her and he wouldn't get paid, and those who would have paid him would make sure he incurred their wrath. Policemen and government thugs working privately were not people he cared to upset. "Let me get back my concentration and see what else I can find out for you," he said hopefully.

He closed his eyes, saw indistinct images, heard vague whispers, sensed strange pulses, and felt as though his consciousness was being sucked away. The experience was far more unusual and interesting than normal, yet its disturbing nature and the circumstances under which it was operating made him wish it wasn't happening.

Wherever this girl finally ended up, she would be in grave danger, but from whom was a mystery. It didn't feel like those who wanted her now, and although she'd mentioned her parents, it didn't feel like them, either. It felt like strangers. And there was her baby, giving out an energy that guided her, as though it sought reunion through a final confrontation between her and those who had stolen it.

He shook his head. It was too much to grasp, and too weird, even for him. He looked at Sarah, hoping she might have drank her tea. She hadn't, and he wondered what those watching intended to do now their plan had faltered.

"You have had a most distressing life," he said.

A gruff voice stirred from its slumber within Sarah's head and said, "For fuck's sake get on with it or leave. This silly bastard is getting on my nerves."

Sarah stiffened.

Azad glanced around with a startled expression. "Who was that?" He scanned the courtyard. "I heard an intruder uttering foul insults."

"It was one of my voices," she informed him. "One of the nasty ones."

He looked wildly at her. "What?"

"I'm schizophrenic and I sometimes hear voices in my head. That was one of the regular ones."

Azad tried to compose himself but found it difficult. He hadn't expected such a development - telepathic at that. It was frightening, something new, and that it had happened with a lunatic made it even more terrible.

"It is cruel," he said. "Why do you allow it to talk this way?"

"I have no control over it, or any of the others. They come and go whenever they like. My medicine helps to keep them away for a lot of the time, but they always find a way to sneak back."

"It must be an evil spirit." He stood up, scanned the doors around the courtyard, wishing something would happen, and moved away on the pretext of inspecting a plant. "Have you considered exorcism?" He knew an exorcist and under normal conditions would have pursued the idea on a commission basis. Now he was simply killing time.

Sarah recalled a television programme about exorcisms in America, used in pseudo-religious brainwashing scams to indoctrinate gullible fools or those with mental problems. She had even seen a born-again evangelist type at Speaker's Corner in Hyde Park ranting about serpents in his belly and evil spirits in his head. She'd had no doubt that he was schizophrenic or round the twist in some other way. And now she had Azad hovering before her, looking less benevolent and a lot more sinister.

"I think it's time I left," she said, and as she stood up a creeping shadow completed its attack and engulfed half the courtyard. The sun had finally slipped behind an adjacent building, and as if by magic three men appeared ominously before her, their faces hard, eyes watchful. She jumped up in alarm, recognized one of them as Ravi. "What do you want?" she shouted at him.

"Please stay calm," he replied. "We have no wish to harm you."

"What do you want then?"

He closed in, the other two flanking him. "We only want to keep you safe for a little while. Please do as we say."

"It will be best if you obey," Azad said with a noticeable trace of relief, "otherwise you will be in trouble."

Ravi shot him a disproving glance and smiled unconvincingly at Sarah.

"You have nothing to fear," he reassured her.

"Why do you want me?" she asked angrily. "What's all this about?" She swayed on the balls of her feet, her hands waiting fists. Energy throbbed in her arms and legs, and her nose filled with the smell of old curry. When realization dawned, she said, "You're the bastards who stole my baby - aren't you?"

"No. We are here to help you find the people who did," Ravi said softly. "We are your friends." He smiled, laid a hand on her arm. "We know who they are and where to find them. Come, we'll show you."

"Show you death," warned Sarah's gruff voice. "Death and destruction and the very pits of Hell. Kill 'em and be damned."

Ravi took her left arm, expecting no resistance. When she pulled it away he grabbed it tightly and said, "Do not resist."

"Fuck you," and she caught him on the temple with a right hook, following it with several more, forcing him to let go. As one of the other men grabbed her right arm she stuck her thumb in his eye and kneed him in the crotch, the third man lunging forward, his arms closing around her in a bear-hug. She screamed abuse into his face, and as he lifted her kicked his legs violently. He tightened his grip with a curse, squeezed the air from her lungs. In a desperate bid to be free she bit down hard on his nose.

The man screamed, dropped her, staggered back. Ravi threw a punch as she fell against the divan and rolled into the fish pond. He came after her in a straight line, the man she'd kneed circling to her right, Azad with the mute girl, both watching with mounting horror.

"Come on you cunt," Sarah screamed, "and I'll kill you kill you kill you kill you," and she shot forward, pushed Ravi off the edge of the pond and into the divan. He bounced off, sprawled on the floor, smashed the cup. Sarah landed on top of him, pounded at his face until the man with the bitten nose dragged her off.

Her voices screamed like harpies, their frenzy contagious. Sarah drew strength, found the man's testicles and squeezed. He released her with a yell, aimed a punch, missed as she darted away, the third man intercepting. She smashed him in the face without slowing and made it to the front door, bolt forgotten, and beat her fist against it.

"Open this fuckin' door," she shouted at it.

A sound behind made her turn. It was Ravi, the whites of his eyes glowing in the darkened vestibule. She snatched an incense holder off the wall, leapt forward and swung it at his head. He ducked, lashed out, missed and went down with a groan as Sarah caught him off-balance, the holder impacting across the crown of his head. He tried to crawl away as she hit him again and again until a soft unfamiliar voice in her head urged her to stop. Puzzled, she looked up and saw the girl standing by the door which led into the courtyard.

"You?"

The girl moved to the front door, pulled back the bolt. The harsh noise heightened Sarah's anger and she struck the door with the holder. The girl shook her head, took the holder, placed it carefully on the floor. Sarah glanced into the courtyard, suspicious of the sudden lull. Azad stood in the middle looking completely bewildered. The man with the bitten nose sat on the floor, blood over his face and shirt. The other man stood watching her, his stance suggesting he'd given up. When Ravi groaned beside her she kicked him in the stomach.

"That's for lying to me," she said, and kicked him again.

The door creaked open behind her. Something touched her elbow, causing her to spin round with a raised fist. The girl stared impassively at her, pointed to the alley, stepped out, and gestured for her to follow.

Outside Sarah sucked in air, squeezed pond water from her clothes, and made a mental note to take another pill when she got back to her room. The door slammed shut, irking her, and she followed the girl down the alley, now filled with an unhealthy yellow-grey light that reminded her of hepatitis. No faces peered at her this time, and she wondered if Azad and Ravi and their friends had killed them all.

"You know English?" she asked the girl.

A nod.

"Those men back there, they're bad men?"

A shrug.

"They must be bad otherwise they wouldn't try and steal

me like they stole my baby. You know?"

Another shrug.

Shit, it was like communicating with an alien. Sarah gritted her teeth, angry with her muteness. "You must know who they are?"

The girl shook her head.

"Why are you helping me?"

No response.

"Is Azad your sugar daddy? Do you sleep with him?"

Still no response. Sarah wouldn't have been surprised if that was the case. The old cunt was probably a lecher under his smooth disguise. All mumbo-jumbo men were. It was just another power trip to join all the others. But who were those men and what did they want? It obviously had something to do with her baby, otherwise there was no point to it. But how did they know about it? Maybe bitch-mother had been here and told them about it, showed it to them. Couldn't have been her father because no money was mentioned. Obviously mother had the baby and wanted her to abort the mission, Ravi and his goons on hand to make sure she did. Well, she showed them, and now she knew the baby was in India. Or maybe it wasn't - but something had to be otherwise the star signal wouldn't have given her instructions. Whatever it was all about, it was clearly dangerous to stay in Delhi. They'd only try and kidnap her again - or did they really want to kill her? Shit, it was too much to get her head around.

They passed a bony cow chewing up a cardboard box, entered a road that led to the main street. Sarah lagged behind so she could watch the sylph-like sway of the girl's body. When she smelt sweet jasmine she thought of sex, but not for long. The main street appeared and rush hour din took over.

A tuk-tuk bounced towards them. The girl waved it down. Sarah climbed in and nearly climbed straight back out. The driver was the Sikh and he laughed at her expression. This wasn't co-incidence, Sarah told herself, this was the result of an intelligence network, probably Azad's. He could no more read her mind than she could talk to a dolphin. The old cunt was a charlatan. Everything he knew about her had been obtained from his spies. He probably had them everywhere, even in Acton, Portugal and Paris, all over the world. Bastard.

She told the Sikh her destination. The girl put her hands together, bowed her head. Sarah did the same, wishing she could somehow get to know her better. The girl smiled, waved, walked away. Sarah leaned out of the tuk-tuk and watched her. It wasn't fair that such a beautiful girl should be so awkwardly afflicted. Maybe Azad had cut out her vocal cords at birth and used them for shoelaces. There had to be another way she could communicate apart from nodding and shaking her head, using signs and mimes and presumably writing on bits of paper like a well-trained chimp.

Down the road the girl suddenly turned and looked back. It was then that Sarah found out there was another way, and the soft sensuous voice, melodic as a songbird, brought tears to her eyes. Then the girl vanished in the crowds, the tuk-tuk swung out into traffic, and Sarah's mind filled with junk.

8

FALSE AFFINITY

Melissa Burnham walked hurriedly to her car, unlocked the driver's door and opened it. Before she could get in someone tapped her on the shoulder. Startled, she turned quickly and faced a smiling well-dressed woman who looked vaguely familiar.

"Hello. Going off to spy on Alan?"

Melissa's face went blank. "Sorry?"

"I'd like to talk to you about something we have in common."

Melissa eyed her warily, said nothing.

"Do you have a few minutes to spare?"

"No. I'm busy." She half-turned but didn't attempt to get in the car.

"But you're nevertheless interested."

Melissa faced her with a surprisingly hostile expression. "No I'm not. Now will you leave me alone, I'm late for an appointment."

"My name's Janet, and I'm here because we're both having trouble with men."

"Speak for yourself. I never have trouble with them."

Because you can't fucking get them, you drab little bitch. Janet kept her smile, said, "What about Alan Raddick?"

"Who's he?"

"Surely you haven't forgotten the psychiatrist who tried to rape you?"

Melissa stood perfectly still, face lifeless. Even her eyes resembled those of a dead person.

Such a telling defence, thought Janet.

"I know you haven't forgotten him," she continued, "because you've been watching him since his release from prison."

"You've got the wrong person."

Janet moved closer, her countenance darkening. "I don't think so, Melissa."

Melissa pressed back against the car, heart accelerating. "Look, I don't know what you're talking about or who this Alan Raddish is. You've obviously got the wrong person, so please step back and let me get into my car." She tried to sound assertive but a shrillness betrayed her anxiety. "If you don't I'll call the police."

Janet loomed over her, oozing menace. "His name is Raddick, and please believe me when I tell you that you won't have the chance to call the police." She stepped back, gave her space. "I suggest you stop playing the innocent and pay attention, because I know all about you and Raddick - and your current surveillance of him."

The assertion undermined Melissa's confidence and she felt a twinge of panic. Was she a new girlfriend of Alan's? She glanced up and down the street, fearing public humiliation. The street was deserted, and in that instant emphasized her isolation, and should the woman turn violent, her possible vulnerability.

She looked into the woman's dark eyes and said, "What do you want? Who are you?"

"You want Alan for reasons best known to yourself. I want you to have him for reasons that will become apparent. I can help you, and in turn you can help me. Understand?"

"No, I don't." Janet's face nagged at her memory but she couldn't place her. "Have we met before?"

"Our paths crossed a few years ago in Kingston Psychiatric Unit."

Melissa recalled seeing her, and said, "But you weren't a patient?"

"No. My daughter, Sarah, was there. She's schizophrenic."

"I remember her." Surly slut trying it on with Alan in his office, thinking I wouldn't know, refusing my presence like she was the Queen of Sheba. "How is she now?"

"Seriously unwell."

"I'm sorry to hear that."

"Thank you. Now I think it's time we went to your room for a chat."

"I don't know about that. I mean - ." She scrutinized Janet's face, finding within the entrenched bitterness of her eyes and mouth a maleficent hardness that made her even more wary. "It's scruffy and - how do you know I've got a room?"

"Lock the car, Melissa, and let's go and have a chat. I haven't got a lot of time."

Melissa reluctantly did as she was told, Janet's assertive manner putting her on edge.

"How do you know about me?" she asked as they walked to the terraced house where her room was located.

"I've been watching you closely," Janet replied.

Melissa clenched her teeth, stopped at the front door. A lava flare from within heated her skin, made her draw breath. What else had this woman been doing? Had she taken up with Alan and this was all part of a plan to harm her? Cut her up, throw acid in her face, perhaps even kill her?

She turned and said, "I've changed my mind. We can talk here."

Janet hid her surprise, put on a mask of concern, glanced up and down the street like a self-conscious conspirator. "I don't know if that's a good idea, Melissa. You never know who might be listening with directional mikes and all that spy stuff." Melissa glanced up and down the street. "Oh, I'm sorry," Janet continued. "I'm jumping ahead of myself. Believe me, it really would be better if we talked inside. And I'm sorry if I came on a bit strong earlier. That wasn't my intention. I'm under a lot of pressure at the moment. I have problems to sort out and very little time to do anything, which is why I need your help if we are to save Alan."

The last two words worked wonders. Melissa stiffened like the recipient of an electric shock. "Save Alan? From what?"

"It's a little complicated. Can we go inside?"

Melissa's room was on the first floor. It was small, sparsely furnished, without personal items other than those consumables necessary for living. The absence of personality suggested to Janet that Melissa led a fluid life, unable to stay in one place for long, put down roots, acquire substance, either material or social. It was the room of a person imprisoned in their own mind and on the run from life.

"Sarah is in India," Janet commenced without preamble, "sick and out of control. My husband - who I'm in the process of divorcing - is the person you've seen Alan meet while you've been watching him. He wants to murder Sarah so he can get the money from her life insurance policy. He's planning this with Alan, knowing he's down on his luck and needs some money."

The news shocked Melissa, and several seconds passed before she spoke.

"That's terrible. How can Alan stoop so low?"

"He tried to rape you, didn't he?"

"Yes, but murder....."

"I know what you mean. It's shocking, but the facts speak for themselves."

"I'm surprised Alan's involved in this. I know he's got problems and needs someone to keep him on the straight and narrow, but murder......" She shook her head.

Oh what twisted love you have, Melissa, and Janet said, "I think my husband is exerting a bad influence over him, either forcing him to help or not telling him the true extent of his plans. You know what men are like; so two-faced, even with each other."

"Don't I just."

"Of course, otherwise you wouldn't be living like you do - and I can sympathize. I've also had a bad time at the hands of men, which is why I've come to see you. I want you to help me save my daughter and free Alan from my husband's influence. If we succeed then I can make sure Sarah is looked after properly and you can get Alan back on line; and of course we can ensure that justice is served on my husband."

Janet wondered if she was going too fast, or being too emotive, but Melissa seemed to be genuinely attentive.

"What do you want me to do?"

"Come to India with me. It's our only chance."

"India is a long way away." She had never been further than Europe, and India was as appealing as Pluto. She immediately pictured Janet murdering her in some stink-filled backstreet full of disease and rotting garbage. "Can't the police out there help you?"

"My husband has bribed them into helping him. Same with the British embassy and detective agencies. He's got everyone in his pocket."

"So what can we do against so many people, especially if your husband is as evil as you suggest. He might have the police arrest us, torture us or something worse."

"Evil he is, but he's not as cunning as women can be when their backs are against the wall, especially women like us. I have money and I can pay the police and others more than he's paid them, so we'll be in the strongest position, not him. I think my daughter is certainly worth that - and Alan, too. Already they're on their way out there."

Melissa straightened abruptly. "What? Alan's already on his way? To India? Now?"

"Yes. They sneaked off last night on a direct flight to Delhi. I only found out after they'd gone."

It was a lie. She'd found out two hours after Bill's meeting with Raddick, when he had telephoned British Airways from his office and booked two first class tickets on the evening flight. Her agency had e-mailed her a transcript of the call, together with one of a call he'd made to an Indian embassy official. She had reacted quickly, driven more by anger than cunning.

Boosting her fees to the agency, she'd managed to arrange for Sarah to be abducted by their contacts out there, and held captive until she decided what to do next. It had been short notice to say the least, which is perhaps why she had received news only hours later that the stupid bastards had cocked it up and Sarah had escaped. Worse than that, she'd left Delhi almost immediately after and the stupid fools hadn't bothered to follow her. Now she had two tickets of her own to Delhi, with a different airline, leaving in a matter of hours.

For a while Melissa stood looking out the window. Eventually she turned to Janet and said, "Have they landed yet?"

"Yes. I suppose they'll hunt Sarah down and have her killed, unless my husband does it himself. Or manages to talk Alan into doing it."

"I can't imagine Alan doing such a thing."

"My husband is evil incarnate. He'd cut up his own mother if he thought there was money in it. He's beaten me enough times."

Melissa winced with unpleasant memories. "Alan must be totally under your husband's influence. I just can't imagine him doing all this of his own accord." She frowned reflectively. "What I don't understand is how he could be so heavily influenced. He's always struck me as far too individualistic."

You mean self-centred, thought Janet. "Perhaps his time in prison changed him," she said softly. "It must have been tough for him, bearing in mind some of the mindless animals he was locked up with."

"Yes, you're probably right. No one can come out of that the same as they went in."

"Exactly, so it stands to reason that he needs someone like you to help him back to normality, to guide him into a way of life even better than what he had before he went inside."

A faint smile struggled across Melissa's face. "Yes, men often need a guiding hand, like children really - which is what they basically are."

"Yes, I think you're right." Janet paused for just the right number of seconds before asking, "So will you help me, Melissa? Please?" The last word slipped out with surprising ease, but forging the pitiful expression that went with it was more difficult.

"Yes, of course."

Janet looked relieved. "Good. We leave in six hours. Do you have a valid passport?"

"Yes."

"Give it to me and I'll get the visa done." Using her agency contacts yet again. "I'll be back here in four hours to pick you up."

Melissa leaned across to a drawer, took out her passport, handed it to Janet who flicked through it. It looked unused, the photograph so awful it resembled a weirdly human rodent rather than a person. No wonder she was so disturbed, Janet thought, as she snapped it shut.

"Do you have any passport-sized photos I can use for the visa?"

"No, I'm sorry."

"Not to worry, I can get copies made from the one in the passport."

"It's not a very good picture of me."

"You want to see mine," Janet responded with a laugh. "It's gross."

"What shall I pack?"

"It's hot in India, so take it from there."

"What about injections and malaria tablets?"

"Hopefully we won't be staying there long enough to catch

anything."

"Oh, I thought we might have time for some sightseeing."

Jesus Christ, Janet thought angrily, what did she think this was, a fucking school trip?

"If everything works out okay we could stop off on the way back, perhaps in the Seychelles, get a tan - yes?"

"Sounds lovely, but there is one thing. What about spending money? The cost of the ticket? How much do I owe you?"

Janet shook her head. "You owe me nothing. I'm only too happy to have you by my side." She dipped into her handbag, found her purse, took out a hundred pounds in twenties. "Take this in case you need to get anything before we go."

"Thank you," Melissa said, taking the notes.

"Once I get the money for the trip sorted out I'll give you some more." She stood up, held out a firm hand. "I'm glad we had the opportunity to become friends."

"So am I," Melissa confirmed, weakly shaking her hand. "And I really do hope we can sort everything out."

"So do I. I'll see myself out." And you too, once we've finished in India.

Melissa watched from the window as Janet walked down the garden path and into the street. A wry smile contorted her features. Yes, Janet dear, I'll help you find that surly diseased daughter of yours, and once we've found her - she screwed up the twenty pound notes in her hand - the whore-faced bitch will be the least of your troubles.

9

ECHOES

Bill and Raddick had been in their Delhi hotel for less than ten minutes when a diminutive Indian gentleman turned up unannounced and introduced himself simply as Dua, Bill's main agency representative in the city. When he told them about the attempt to kidnap Sarah, Bill launched such an intense tirade at Dua that Raddick feared he would end up throttling the man.

"At least she got away," he said, trying to calm him. "Mr Dua's team can't be blamed for something they had no knowledge of at the time."

"I know that," Bill retorted, "but if Janet's people had succeeded who knows what would have happened - and thanks to them Sarah's now bolted to Varanasi, which makes our job a lot more difficult."

"With due respects, Mr Donaldson," said the diminutive Dua, "I think if you stay here for tonight things will not look so grim tomorrow. My men are following your daughter most closely, with orders to keep watch for others who might be interested in her. Already I have told them to make sure nothing happens to her and she is not interfered with. I have every confidence in - ."

"For God's sake shut up about who or what you have confidence in, because frankly I don't have confidence in anything you're doing - and in view of what I'm paying you I should have. If they had succeeded in kidnapping Sarah - what then? Or say they had killed her - what would you have done then, Dua? Uh? Given me a refund? I want results, not excuses. Understand?"

Dua nodded humbly, knowing that despite the absence of information about the other party's interest in Sarah Donaldson, he could have organized things a little better. And in view of how much could still be earned from this assignment, he would make sure that all future possibilities were covered.

Dua said, "Tomorrow I can have a very comfortable car ready to take you to Varanasi."

"If she's still there," Bill snapped back.

"We could make leaving difficult for her," Dua suggested.

"She's schizophrenic for Christ's sake - do you know what that is?"

"An unfortunate illness of the mind. I have been briefed by my head office in London regarding its unpredictability."

"Like the other lot no doubt, and it didn't do them much good."

Dua moved his head ambiguously. "Your daughter put up a most spirited defence, Mr Donaldson."

"Which is probably how you found out about the kidnap attempt, the injuries inflicted by Sarah such a good laugh that news of it spread like wildfire."

"With due respects, Mr Donaldson, we did not greet the news with amusement. Far from it, in fact. Apart from its failure the only point for which we can be thankful is that your wife's henchmen are amateurs."

Bill ran his fingers through his hair. Dua was irritating him beyond toleration. "You have people watching the airport and liaising with London in case my wife comes here?"

"Yes sir."

"And you have people monitoring the activities of her agency people in case she uses them again?"

"Yes sir."

Bill looked at his watch. "Ten o'clock," he announced to no one in particular. "I feel like I've been here for days." He looked at Raddick. "What do think, Alan? Shall we leave

Varanasi until tomorrow?"

Raddick looked at Dua. "How long does it take to drive there?"

"Impossible to say with any worthwhile accuracy, but at least ten or more hours, depending on the state of the road and the amount of traffic. It is a long way, about eight hundred kilometres, or five hundred miles. It can often take over twelve hours by express train."

Raddick addressed Bill. "If we leave now we might get there by midnight, then we'll be ready for action tomorrow morning. If we don't go until tomorrow then we'll be running as good as a day late."

"By which time Janet could be India, maybe in Varanasi. I'm sure she'll come here now that her plan has failed - and I bet she only did that in a panic because she found out we were coming here. She must have my office phone bugged, damn her."

More speculation, mused Raddick, but it sounded believable. "Can we fly to Varanasi?" he asked Dua.

"There is a private airstrip some miles from the city, but arranging an aeroplane quickly may prove difficult."

"Do it," Bill ordered, "as quickly as possible, and add it to my account. I'm damned if I'm going to spend half a day stuck in a bloody car or train."

"I will do my best, Mr Donaldson, but please appreciate that this is India and we have yet to graduate to the same level of efficiency as your own country. If there is nothing more I will go and attend to the transport."

After Dua had left, Raddick asked Bill if he wanted a drink.

"Yes, several." He looked around his hotel room. "Better than I thought it would be. How's yours?"

"Pretty good. How about we freshen up and meet in the bar in an hour? I doubt Dua will have a plane fixed by then."

"I'll be surprised if he can fix it at all." Bill paused

89

thoughtfully. "Damn Janet. She's really coming into her own, isn't she? What do you think we should do if she turns up?"

"Wait and see what she does."

"By then it might be too late."

'I doubt it.' Raddick opened the door. 'I'll see you downstairs."

Bill watched him close the door before sitting back and staring at the ceiling.

India. Strangers trying to kidnap Sarah. His wife a psychopath. He could scarcely believe it. It was like a film, a fiction that had no place in reality. At least Sarah had seen off her assailants with the strength of the mad. Thank God for that. For a moment he tried to imagine what she looked like, and cursed not getting photographs taken by Dua's people. Maybe later. Maybe not at all.

His mind travelled back to a fourteen year old girl who had the blueprint for a successful life etched on every facet of her appearance. She stood 5' 5", had long brown hair that in the sun revealed a chestnut sheen, and her viridescent eyes sparkled with life. Her complexion was as flawless as nature could make it. When she spoke it was with intelligence.

Sarah painted surreal landscapes and strange mythical creatures, composed poetry and wrote short stories. She had gone on to pass eight GCSEs, securing six A and two B grades. She began A-levels in Art and English, and curious about foreign cultures beyond the increasing uniformity of Europe, Geography. He had never doubted that she would attain top grades and go on to university, a complacency that had haunted him ever since.

Little had he realized that beneath his daughter's eruditeness and elegance, attractive demeanour and thoughtful composure, slumbered a malevolent army of genetic propensities, chemical imbalances, distorted memories and twisted interpretations - all awaiting a catalyst. And the catalyst had come. Slowly. Insidiously. Like a well-armed terrorist in the night.

Bill's eyes narrowed as he recalled their encounter.

In recognition of Sarah's artistic talents, her school had held a week-long exhibition of her paintings which was so successful (they all sold) that the headmistress decided to award her a special certificate of distinction. It was to be presented at a formal school presentation.

At first Sarah had appeared elated, but as the presentation drew closer she seemed increasingly depressed and withdrawn. What dark broodings she had fallen into, what twisted logic had been dominating her thoughts, had been a mystery to Bill, until that fateful afternoon when the secret was revealed and he realized just how little he had known about his daughter.

The memory had the clarity of the present, and stung painfully.

Clutching several sheets of paper, Sarah took the stage in the assembly hall to collect her certificate. As the applause died down she took the microphone and gazed at her audience with unblinking eyes which unsettled with their sparkle, their green intensity, their dazzling certainty.

When absolute silence prevailed, she waited. When the silence threatened to engulf parents, students and the school officials sitting behind her in embarrassment, she blinked and smiled, as if sharing a secret joke. Without preamble she launched straight into her acceptance speech, her voice clear and sharp.

"A serious situation exists in this country. Talent is being destroyed while moronic trash is being elevated in society. There is an unconscious desire to isolate and destroy artists, poets, writers and musicians who are a cut above the average. This is gaining momentum and interacts as a reinforcer.

"Large corporations and media monguls are behind it. They cannot be affectively resisted because they use the media tool for conditioning. They work together making soap suds, quinticraptual quiz shows and extreme minority stuff. Radio stations play insane deejays, repetitive news broadcasts and simplistic music not fit for supermarket tills. Advertising companies seduce us with false images and sell things we don't need. Books and magazines aren't worth the paper printed on. All popular music is predominately meritless because we never hear the real thing."

At this point Janet asked Bill what the hell she was talking about.

"Conspiracies," he whispered, sensing something far worse.

Sarah continued. "Hollywood films deprecate on our screens. British films turn them off. Newspapers blind us with the trivia of people's lives while more important issues are pushed to the background with biased lies. Our air, food, water, bodies, minds and souls are being poisoned and we're being charged for it. The reply is pathetic protest and the usual lip-wank of self-surfing politicians. We are overloaded with knowledge. Our heads are spinning. Cities are Babels obscuring the truth so deeply buried in mindless glitz and trash we wouldn't know it if we ate it."

Janet shook her head, whispered, "She's stoned."

"She looked okay in the car."

"Well she's not bloody well okay now, is she?"

Bill looked at the school officials sitting on the stage behind Sarah, saw scowls, perplexity and blank expressions in equal amounts. The headmistress appeared particularly baffled.

"These dirty soul-snatchers are suppressing talent so the mindlessly simplistic status quo can be maintained to benefit balance sheets and rich bastards who end up with millions while millions of others end up homeless and unemployed and have their potential squeezed out like juice from a lemon."

Sarah paused to catch her breath. Parents frowned. Students hung between awe, embarrassment and laughter.

Coughing came from the back of the hall. Someone on stage whispered for her to get off. Janet glared at her.

Undeterred, Sarah carried on. "This potential is the heart of the matter," she shouted, so loudly it was almost deafening. Departing from her speech, she exclaimed, "See! Already you've made the decision not to listen because of your conditioning. You should feel ashamed of this weakness and be like me. I am a talented artist, but all around me subtle forces push me down avenues which have no connection with my soul, my creative essence, what powers me, gives me my talent and fuels my ambitions."

"She's losing it completely," Janet whispered. "Getting wilder by the second. Surely one of those sitting behind her will stop it."

"Maybe I should go up there," Bill suggested.

"Rather you than me."

Sarah roared on, expletives filling her tirade. From behind her came an angry command to shut up, then a hand gripped her shoulder, pulled her back. It was a head teacher, a steely glint in his eye. He pulled the microphone from her hand, attempted to speak. She snatched it back, waved it threateningly at him. The headmistress rose from her chair, closed in. Sarah danced along the stage, identifying the threats springing up around her.

"What's the matter?" she shouted into the microphone. "Think some piece of paper is gonna make me grovel at your feet? Fuck you! I don't need your poxy school with its poxy -"

Janet closed her eyes. Bill stood, deeply embarrassed but mindful that he had to do something. He worked his way along the row of seats, determined not to make eye contact with anyone. By the time he reached the aisle Sarah was ranting uncontrollably as the headmistress and two teachers tried to wrestle the microphone from her.

"You bastards are all the same," she screamed. "I know,

I've heard it from those who bleed in space watching us destroy ourselves. And if - ."

Bill glanced back at Janet, hoping forlornly for some support. She sat with her eyes still closed. People stared at her. Then she opened her eyes and stared straight ahead, face flushed, seeing yet not seeing, until she, too, rose and followed him. He continued to the stage, climbed it like Everest, and the next thing he knew he was grappling with his daughter, her hair a mess, her green eyes wild as her strength outstripped the sane and became a weapon of the mad.

By the time Sarah had been manhandled off the stage, Janet was at the back of the hall. She stared darkly at him as he force-marched Sarah out of the hall in an act as humiliating as it was sobering. She offered no help at all, not even words of reassurance or comfort. She simply stared with dark eyes as menacingly lifeless and evil as those of a shark or goat.

Bill sat up. Some presentation. And afterwards, during the post mortem in the lounge, Janet had said, "One of her teachers wanted to talk to us after the presentation because he was concerned about Sarah's work. That makes me fear the worst. I'd go back there now if I wasn't feeling so damned embarrassed by it all. Did you see the look the Hendersons gave us as we left? And the Framptons. All of them, the whole damned assembly. God knows if the school will have her back."

Janet was always concerned about the family's reputation at Sarah's school, about the neighbours, any embarrassment which never really did seem to affect her. Maybe Raddick had been right and nothing - even her family, friends and home - affected her in the slightest, because she was simply spinning an image to appease her egocentricity, and as long as everything looked good to others she could continue to infiltrate and manipulate.

For Sarah, he later found out, that year had been particularly bad, yet neither he nor Janet had seen the signs for what they really were, thinking instead they were just the normal ups and downs of being a teenager. From the death flare of early summer to the cremation of autumn, she had become increasingly fragmented. Brittle thin, as befitted the illusion that unrealistic expectations can spawn. Her disintegration had accelerated, her imagination exploding in all directions, its expression increasingly chaotic as fantasy and reality became further entwined, and paranoia slinked in unchallenged. Matters had reached a head in December not only with the speech, but the fight afterwards with Janet, when she discovered that Sarah's bedroom had taken on the appearance of one of her paintings, an abstract entitled 'The Colours of Fruit Squatting in a Bedroom.' It had sold for £150.

What Bill had felt when he'd walked into her bedroom struck him again, despite being in India a few years down the line. His hotel room lost substance as Sarah's bedroom invaded time and space and came back to haunt him with the bizarre and tragic ugliness so inherent in the beauty of the mad. It struck him with such a profound sense of dislocation that his head spun. The walls, ceiling and furniture screamed at him like flat-faced harpies whose wrath came in colours. Sarah's consumables littered every surface. Clothes laid everywhere, remnants of a great orgy. Plants on the window sill leaked dirty water. The wardrobe doors hung open. Strange symbols and blotches nagged at his eyes. An easel and canvases stood lopsided in a corner, palettes and paint discarded on the carpet before them. Perfume, paint and old cigarette smoke clogged his nose. A laundry basket stood up-ended, incense sticks lodged between burnt wicker. The thought that he had the wrong room in the wrong house in the wrong life flashed horribly through his mind.

Then he was back in his hotel room and similar thoughts came again.

10

DOG BIRTH

A young man in a white robe picked up a wizened brown arm and tossed it into spitting flames. For a moment they shrunk away, then reared voraciously and ate into the tough thin flesh.

Sarah wondered if the bereaved man knew that the arm and the body it belonged to would never burn on the moon. The notion made her glance up at a hazy sky and catch the mid-morning sun. With a shock she realized that despite its distance, parts of it had arrived on earth long ago and continued to live on the planet, sprouting like weeds, eating with relish, scouring for more and scouring what it found, until only black and grey ashes were left.

The man walked round the pyre, pushing loose wood into the flames. When he reached the end that pointed to an adjacent river, he paused in deliberation, then picked up a long piece of scented wood from the ground and smashed his father's skull into several pieces. Flames roared angrily and licked the bone, tongued the bubbling brains, spat ash, flecking the son's robe and newly-shaven head.

Smelling sandalwood, Sarah let her gaze be drawn by the other funeral pyres. Dr. Raddick would like it here: there was much food for thought; much cathartic worth in smashing the head of a despised relative under the guise of a funereal rite. A funeral necessity: to appease the flames of the sun, and with the congealed ashy excrement, appease the turbid river that was the Ganges. She grinned. Why argue with family when you can wait until they die, then bring them to the burning ghats and smash their bones and watch them burn burn burn?

She laughed. A short vicious laugh with an edge like a cut-throat razor waved in the face. A laugh no one could share, only walk quickly away from.

At one of the pyres, ashes coagulated with fat were being collected and thrown without ceremony into the uneasy brown river. At another, wood was being piled ready for another farewell. As Sarah leaned over the wall of the observation balcony, she heard, directly below her, the low murmur of grief, and above it, raised voices warning people to get out of the way. Another procession came into view. Another home-made stretcher with a body swathed in brightly-coloured cotton sheets bedecked with flowers. Another bizarre Egyptian-like mummy, its pyramid a pyre, its entombment one of fire and water, its immortality a sludge at the bottom of the Ganges.

Bereaved women in colourful saris surrounded the men who surrounded the body that on shoulders and in death exercised an aloofness worthy of the reverence reserved for saints. The women stopped at the entrance to the ghats, forbidden to go further, and watched the men continue.

Sarah turned away, unimpressed with their grief, indifferent to the fact that like most families intent on despatching the remains of their loved ones into the river at Varanasi, the holiest of Hindu cities, they had travelled hundreds of miles for the privilege at an expense they could ill-afford.

Crows circled the waterfront, their cawing circling inside her skull. Long-boats cut up and down the river. Incomprehensible conversations and indefinable smells clustered around her. Paranoia hovered beyond perception, waiting like a dark mood in the fabric of her surroundings.

A shrill voice cut through the humid dustiness like a scythe.

"This is death. The cleansing of life. The suffocation of water. The deceit of family. Find your child, for he is here, in need of you, his mother."

The gruff voice added, "She's no mother, otherwise the little tart wouldn't be here."   .

Sarah flinched, took a deep breath, remembered the relief she carried in her trouser pocket but almost in the same instant forgot it, instead becoming aware of another presence, this time physical, standing beside her. It was an Indian teenager, and he spoke as she turned to him.

"See the women?" He pointed down at them. "The bracelets on their wrists are different colours, and each colour means something special. Did you know that?"

Sarah stared at his face, into his sharp black eyes, and turned away without replying.

"My name is Jawa," he continued as he sat on the wall and stared at her. "It's short for Jawaharlal. I am a student."

When Sarah didn't respond he shifted his position so that he could see more of her face, and continued staring, willing her to look at him. He saw skin the colour of a dirty suntan; short brown hair chopped rather than cropped; eyebrows in need of replucking; unnaturally bright green eyes that hinted at a secret conflict; a silver nose stud; a thin mouth that curved slightly down. None of these turned fully in his direction.

"You are German?" he said with a touch of annoyance.

Sarah gazed at the river, her eyes focused on the grey back of a large fish breaking the surface. Jawa followed her gaze. Her silence and peculiar composure intrigued him - challenged him - and he sought another approach.

"You can get a boat to travel the river," he said.

"A boat ride to Hell," said the shrill voice.

"Everyone burns at the end," Sarah said in a monotone.

That she had finally spoken gave Jawa the encouragement he needed. He took what she had said as a question and replied, "Not everyone. Holy men and very young children are tied to rocks and put in the river."

Sarah spun abruptly and faced him. "Did you say

children?"

Her sudden agitated tone startled him. He wasn't sure if it signified urgency or outrage. He nodded and shrugged, as if to say, this is India. It is our way.

She turned her back to him, paused, then walked away. A myriad of thoughts rushed in and out of her head and after several steps she stopped, anxious to do something but too confused to know precisely what.

"Your child holds the river as the river holds the child," said the shrill voice. "River of life, river of death. Boats are souls where passage is gained."

"Boat the river," added the gruff voice. "With luck you might drown and join your precious child."

"My child's alive," Sarah shouted.

"If it was you wouldn't be here, you stupid little slag."

Her face contorted and she gripped her head, oblivious to the curious stares of those around her. Jawa appeared beside her.

"You are not well?" he asked with genuine concern.

His voice sounded so loud that it rang like a bell in her head. She rubbed her temples vigorously, felt the unavoidable dust on her skin, blocking her pores, penetrating, filling her tubes and organs and the spaces between them. She shuddered and turned to him.

"Can people talk with a mouthful of dust?"

Jawa frowned, glanced at her thin arms, saw no needle marks, and shrugged. Maybe she'd been smoking, he thought, but dismissed the notion. Her movements were too abrupt, too angst-ridden. Perhaps she was what the western junkies who lived on the houseboats called an acid casualty.

"My baby is alive, you know."

Jawa nodded gravely, as if he fully understood what was troubling her. "You would like a boat trip on the river?" he said hopefully. "I can arrange it."

River-water-boat-child: Sarah gave a brief smile, and for a

moment Jawa saw a flash of tenderness.

"Yes," she said. "You sort it out. You must be my guide. I'll call you Charon and together we'll sail the Styx."

"My name is Jawa," he reminded her. "Please follow me."

"Names are just labels to help the forgetful. I don't have a name."

Jawa glanced uneasily over his shoulder. He had met some crazy westerners during his periods of hustling, but this one had a distinct edge he couldn't quite identify. Still, she made a change from the usual type, and if she had money.....

He led her to a narrow street behind the observation balcony. It teemed with merchants, the bereaved, beggars, the unemployed and a host of others. He kept close to Sarah's side so she wouldn't stray.

Colours, sounds, smells and movement swept into her, overwhelming her thoughts and driving them away. The more she bathed her mind in the sensory input, the more Jawa became irrelevant. Only when he stopped outside a tiny shop adorned with badly made metal souvenirs and took her arm did she remember him.

"My uncle's shop," he stated with false pride. "Please come and look."

River-water-boat-child: Sarah glanced around. "Where's the river? I can't see it." Her voice was ragged with a growing panic.

"It is close. Please, come in for a minute. My uncle is a very fair man."

Sarah glared angrily at him. "Fuck your uncle!" A shrivelled old man with a huge basket of chapatis bumped into her. She glared at him, too, her anger intensifying, burning her insides. "You said you'd take me to the river. Get a boat." A smelly cocktail of piss, sweat, river and garbage fuelled her mood. "You lied to me!" Sari reds and greens hugged her retinas. "You're all the same," she shouted as Indian dialects drilled into her head and the incomprehensible became clear.

"You're all trying to stop me reach the river, and don't say you're not because I can hear you," and with wild eyes she turned in circles glaring at everyone within eye contact. "You're all trying to stop me finding the truth." She homed in on Jawa. "But I can afford it. I can buy you and the truth!" and she pulled a wad of banknotes from her moneybelt. "See? Rupees! Thousands of them!"

More heads turned, more eyes became attentive. Jawa gestured for her to put the money away, his own eyes alert for snatch-thieves.

"Okay, okay," he soothed. "We go to the river now. No problem."

He led her along an alley slimy with filth and mud, and down a flight of stone steps smoothed by a million feet. At the bottom a pair of mongooses frolicked, tied by leads to their owner's hole-in-the-wall cake shop. Sarah paused, thinking their captivity significant, and tried to stroke them until one nearly removed a finger. She called the owner a plague-ridden bastard and without being conscious of what immediately followed, found herself by the river's edge.

She scanned water as brown as tea; scanned small circular bathing ghats at the end of short stone walkways; scanned dark pinnacled temples that rose like cones from beneath the water; scanned the rhythm of the waterfront.

"Where are the boats?" she asked, looking over her shoulder as if they might have been hiding from her. Before Jawa could reply, her thoughts jumped elsewhere and she was seized by a sight that held her spellbound.

From the wall of a building a huge mural of Kali in ashen blue stared down at her with an ambiguity befitting a goddess who represented the ultimate reconciliation of opposites. As Sarah stared at it, Kali's eyes and lips flickered with life.

"Come," urged Jawa. "The boats are this way."

Kali broke the spell with a whisper that made Sarah gasp and turn quickly away.

"What is the matter?" Jawa asked.

"She told me that even dead babies babble."

He glanced around for a woman with a baby, but no women were in talking distance. He scanned the rivers edge for a small corpse, but there was nothing. He dismissed her comment.

"Yes, this way, please."

As Jawa knew the owner of the boat - more a long canoe - and the twelve-year-old oarboy who would do the rowing, he had no compunction in charging Sarah three times the going rate for an hour's hire. Much to his surprise she merely nodded her agreement, more concerned and excited by the search that lay ahead.

Eager to get started she sat on a cross-plank at the bow, the oarboy astern.

"We go down the river to the other burning ghats," Jawa said from behind her. "It will take only a short time."

"Then let's go," Sarah shouted.

As the boat nosed out into the river, the Ganges opened up before her, and she opened up for the Ganges, her eyes darting across the 180-degree vista.

As they passed the burning ghats where Sarah had met Jawa, she turned and asked, "Why don't the bodies smell of burning flesh?"

"Scented wood."

"I said the bodies not the wood."

Jawa frowned. "The same. They dip the body three times in the river and after it has dried they sprinkle scent on it. Then a man relative has to shave his head, wear white, and - ."

"I didn't see anyone sprinkle scent on the bodies," and she turned her back to him. "What's that?" she shouted with sudden agitation, pointing at something in the river. "That there?"

Jawa saw a holy man fixed to a stretcher, his covered head and shoulders visible above the water. He answered her question, adding that the stones to weigh him down must have come loose. When Sarah gave no indication that she had heard him, he looked at the oarboy who smiled at him, and made a gesture suggesting she was crazy.

The boy rowed quietly. The boat moved slowly. Jawa sat glumly. The active waterfront stretched alongside them, only a stone's throw away, and drifted past like a sluggish dream which Sarah absorbed in its entirety, netting sights and sounds by the second, her perceptive filters failing rapidly, her mind ingesting ravenously the sensory input that swarmed around her begging for attention.

And within this morass of input a part of her hunted relentlessly amongst the stony slopes and steep-stepped expanses and dark primary-coloured buildings and busy people for a sign, a clue, a shadow that would confirm the validity of her search, her reason for being in Asia, for stealing her father's slush money and buying an air ticket to India, and for being different, for being chosen.

The waterfront stretched, contracted, came and went and shrieked and murmured: two men cleaning stainless steel pots and pans in the river, the sun glinting off the metal into Sarah's eyes like branding irons on the retinas; women washing clothes and sheets and hanging them on makeshift lines or spreading them out to dry on steps and walls; water buffalo immobile in step-caught dust, their tails flicking flies and messages; breached long-boats dry-docked in death and despair; ashes like turds pushed to land.

It was the beginning of the dry season.

Jawa tapped Sarah on the shoulder. "In the monsoon the river can grow so big all the buildings along here are under water. Big floods. See? On that building, a measuring line."

Sarah saw 60 glaring at her in red from under a warehouse roof and immediately understood what it really meant. She looked 60 feet in front of the building and saw the river licking the gas-bloated grey-white body of a sacred cow.

Close, she thought. Getting close. And the shrill voice said to her, "Close is far in the eternal infinity that is the river of life."

"Shut up," the gruff voice responded. "If you didn't talk such utter shit the silly little bitch would see her godforsaken bitch-bastard son in all his festering glory."

And in that instant Sarah saw it. Further up the river, just past a group of children swimming near the dead cow, oblivious to its stink, its disease, its unholiness.

Jawa saw it, too, and wished he hadn't. Not because it repelled him, but because he feared it would exacerbate the mistaken notion foreigners tended to have about the traditions that made the river such a rich feeding ground for creatures like the Ganges Shark.

As the boat drew parallel to the sight, Jawa waited for Sarah's delayed reactions of shock and outrage. Instead, she moved her whole body so it faced the naked child washed up by the river's edge, and the thin mangy dog that with jaws clamped on a tiny arm was dragging it to dry land.

She pointed at the scene and yelled, "Closer! Take me closer!"

When the boat didn't change direction, she rounded on Jawa with a furious expression and yelled again for the boy to row closer. Jawa flushed darker with embarrassment and anger, and shook his head.

"Tell him to row closer," she shouted, louder this time, and she shouted a fourth time at the oarboy who didn't understand English, then a fifth time at a long-boat passing close by them, vilifying those on board for rocking her boat with distracting bow waves.

"Turn, turn, turn in circles," said the shrill voice, and as the child and dog were left behind Sarah stood and glared at Jawa and the oarboy.

"Turn this fucking boat around - now!" she screamed. "Now! Before I jump off and swim over there!"

Jawa leaned back, muttered a few words to the oarboy, felt the boat wobble from side to side with Sarah's movements, and wondered what he would do if she fell overboard.

As the boat curved round, faced the bank, then straightened up, Jawa told her to sit down. She ignored him and with her back to him, arms akimbo, stared at the child and dog, the children beyond jumping off an old rotting jetty into the filthy river, splashing happily, unconcerned, and beyond them the pallid lump that was the dead cow.

"Faster!" she ordered.

Jawa watched as the dog finished dragging the child from the water. It looked like a boy aged about three, not long in the river, its skin neither discoloured or extended around the abdomen.

"The child is dead," he said unnecessarily.

"The child is always dead," Sarah replied bitterly. "How can a child be otherwise when it's reared by adults?"

Jawa didn't understand and so said nothing.

"I had a child once," Sarah continued, "but they cut it out because they said it was dead inside me. They called it a Caesarean."

"What is a Caesarean?"

"This," and she turned fully to him, pulled up her top and pushed down her trousers until her pubic hair showed. "This is how my baby was stolen from me. They broke into my body like a thief breaks into a house. They drugged me, robbed me, and left me to grieve in pain. Then when I demanded my baby back they drugged me again and took me to a different hospital. One with bars on the window, locks on the door." She turned her back on him as the dog started to bark.

A second dog had appeared, and as they snarled at each other the boat nudged the sloping bank. Sarah jumped down beside the child, looked into fish-eaten eyes and leapt back with a gasp.

"The bastards! They've stolen its eyes so it'll never see its mother."

Jawa stayed on the boat and scratched his head. "Who are they?" he asked, keeping a watchful eye on the dogs.

"They are -." Sarah glanced around. "They are everyone everywhere." She bent and inspected the child. "Is this mine?" she asked herself.

"Right sex," said the shrill voice.

"Wrong colour," said another.

"All babies are born the same colour," she replied. "Blood-red."

"Just like yours are always born dead," chanted several voices, forcing her to her knees and making her cry by the child that wasn't hers.

Jawa looked back at the oarboy and shrugged. The first dog saw off the second and stood salivating as it watched Sarah stroke the sodden hair of its dinner.

"We must go now," Jawa whispered.

The dog snarled.

Sarah stood, her tears ceasing, and regarded the dog with a malign expression as it bared its teeth and moved closer.

"Come," Jawa ordered. "The dog is sick. If it bites you, you have big problem."

But Sarah was oblivious to his advice. In the dog's malevolent hungry eyes she saw the souls of forgotten men, deserting fathers-to-be who never were. Jawa took an oar from the boy and stepped from the boat. The dog sniffed the air, foam drooling over its lower jaw. Flies settled on the loose scabs of its filthy coat. Jawa held the oar ready. Time stopped. The sun's heat turned into a flash of metal table. A searing blade of overhead light wiped out the sky. Bottles, cylinders and machinery clustered around Sarah. Eyes shifted above sinister masks. Plastic hands toyed with instruments of torture. A smell defied analysis. Metallic sounds pierced louder than bells. Everything was simultaneously clear and hazy, distorted and sharp, bright and dim. Muffled voices promising the most terrible violation slid through hot air like dangerous winged creatures.

Then came a gown and gloves; a man with eyebrows crawling over his forehead, eyes dark with a hint of corsair, his nose pointed, mouth tight, lips thin; wearing part of her mother's face, laughing as he sliced, the nurses beaming gargoyle reflections into polished surfaces.

With numbness came awareness: a mistake which shrunk the body, tugged at the soul, froze sensation at the bloody point of an arterial spurt which covered and soaked, filled the air with misty droplets that fell upon the emptying, the disembowelment, the theft that was the lifting of life and brought forth the tang of foetal blood and fear. And the cord, promptly cut, followed by a cry heart-rending in its grief.

A darkness had fallen upon Sarah then, and somewhere in the back of her mind, behind the barricades, she had known that her body would be taken to a secret address stinking of boiled bones and cut up, her dismembered skeleton shipped to a distant land, destined for display in a spartan classroom full of impoverished medical students. Now she had delivered her body personally, and a sick cunt of a dog in front of her was taking the piss, threatening her, threatening her baby and everything women stood for.

"Take the oar," commanded her gruff voice.

Sarah gently placed a hand on the oar then abruptly tried to snatch it from Jawa. "No!" he cried out, tightening his grip. "Get back on the boat."

"Kill it," the gruff voice whispered. "And kill him" - and in a furious burst - "Kill them all, kill them all, kill them all all all!"

The hateful chorus froze her on a path in a muddy wood. She was in remission from her illness and walking with her parents, a Sunday afternoon stroll in the nearby countryside. She asked them if she could have a dog, for company and to take on walks. Her father said it wasn't possible, because her mother had an allergy to dog hair. She looked at her mother who confirmed it. And in that split second it occurred to Sarah that when she was a child she'd once had a dog, a small brown puppy with sad eyes that she'd found sniffing around in the front garden. She had smiled as the cute puppy face with its wet little nose filled her mind's eye, then vanished along with her smile as she recalled why her father had taken it away hours later - too much trouble - needs training - mess on the carpets - damage the furniture - ruin the lawn. Her mother's words, and for an ugly second, as she realized the allergy was a lie, Sarah had made contact with the impression left by the hate she had felt for her parents that day so very long ago, when she'd cried in her room for the best part of an hour until her nanny, Avril, had soothed away the pain as she always did. Or rather had, because she'd committed suicide at the local railway station after being sacked by her mother for smoking dope. The memory had tainted the rest of the walk. And now its echo had returned, doubled in power by another.

Jawa said something incomprehensible.

"Kill the ghosts," Sarah whispered between clenched teeth. "I want to kill the ghosts."

Jawa leaned closer. "Pardon?"

"Give me the fucking oar," and with a surge of strength that surprised him, she snatched it away.

The dog made ready to pounce. Jawa retreated to the boat. The oar swung up and stilled, its broad end pointing at the hazy sky. As the dog attacked, Sarah brought the oar sweeping down and made contact with its head, the sound strangely muffled in the heat murmur of the river. The dog, momentarily stunned, stood stupidly, and she hit it again. And again and again and again, the sounds remaining muffled, her actions detached from her consciousness.

The dog's legs finally gave way. Blood oozed in a line along the top of its head. It looked up at her with puzzled eyes, whimpered, and with a spasm relaxed into the dust. She pushed it into the river with the oar, held it under with a malicious childish glee as bubbles rose to the surface and its legs twitched feebly. It was a weak, sick, hungry dog, she thought, just like the men who had passed through her life. When the bubbles ceased she stepped back on the boat and without so much as a backward glance at the dead child, gave the oar to the stunned boy and sat down. Jawa stared open-mouthed at her.

"I had it wrong," she said with a crooked smile. "I thought my baby would be here; instead it was all my babies' fathers. They had rabies which drives people mad if they get bitten. I suppose that's understandable because dogs are mad anyway."

"We have many mad dogs in India," Jawa said, latching on to the only thing that made any sense to him. "There are many more in Tibet. They are holy animals there, like our sacred cows."

Sarah smiled grimly. "That's a lot of men. How do I get there?"

"From Nepal or China."

"Take me back to the ghats."

He told the oarboy to hurry back, then to Sarah, "You are going to Tibet?"

"No. I'm going east to find my baby."

"Where is it?"

"In the next man who fucks me."

Jawa scratched his head. "Why you talk like this?"

"Because I'm honest but they say I'm sick."

"Who?"

"Everyone, but as long as I take my tablets not sick enough to be kept in hospital. Which is good because hospital is real opal shit."

"What is your sickness?"

"Can't you guess?" She took a small folded piece of paper from her pocket, opened it, and popped two white tablets into her mouth. "These are chlorpromazine. In fifteen minutes my head will clear.

"You treacherous bitch," came a gruff accusation.

Jawa tapped his temple. "You are sick here?"

Sarah smiled, turned away, knowing that the rest of her day - like her life - was mapped out for the moment, the moment lasting as long as her medication would allow. And as the oarboy rowed and the Ganges flowed, she sat in silence listening to her voices rally for a final onslaught before they faded into the hiss of chemical silence.

One shredded her dreams, another her mission, and a third praised her parents; and while the shrill voice assured her that she hadn't had three abortions, the gruff voice insisted that she was controlled by messages beamed into her ear lobes by men whose ghosts were those of every incinerated foetus in the world, which was proof enough of what a slut she was.

Sarah had heard it all before, and waited patiently until one by one they fell silent before their clamour could reach a climax. She giggled then, and turned to Jawa with an endearing smile. He studied her face, and wondered what making love to her would be like.

"You'll never know," she said, thinking how ugly he was.

His eyes widened and she turned away. She had been in Varanasi for two days. Soon she would have to move on, pausing only at those watering holes which dotted the land mass of her mission, and drinking dry the secret signs that hid waiting for her arrival.

11

THE EASTERN MAGNET

The transport arrangements took longer than Dua had anticipated, but eventually he came up with something which eased Bill's impatience. It was an old Lear Jet belonging to an industrialist who kept it solely for sentimental reasons. Apart from occasional family jaunts or emergency use, it was usually kept mothballed in a hanger.

"Never thought I'd be flying over India in an executive jet," Raddick said from across the aisle. "It certainly beats cars or trains."

More bloody expensive, Bill thought moodily, suspecting Dua had hired it for far less than what had been added to his account. He glanced over his shoulder at him, saw only his glossy black hair. He appeared to be dozing, but Bill would have put money on eavesdropping. The little flea, although undoubtedly well-connected and therefore useful, was far too slippery for his tastes; and he'd politely forced him into settling the account before they could step on the plane.

"We're lucky to have Mr Dua helping us," Bill said with a wink. "If it wasn't for him things would be much more difficult."

"They certainly would," Raddick replied with a grin. He looked out his window. The weather was good, only a few clouds obscuring the green and brown of the agricultural Ganges plain that made up most of the north-central state of Uttar Pradesh. "Pity we're not flying closer to the Himalayas," he said. "That would be a sight worth seeing."

"Yes, but not in this plane. The Himalayas are noted for their erratic weather patterns and turbulence."

"How old is the plane? The decor looks very dated."

"I think it was built in the mid-sixties. The owner bought it second-hand in the early seventies. It was the first plane he owned, which is why he still has it. He used it until the eighties when spare parts became difficult to obtain."

"So what does he do now when a part needs replacing?"

"I don't know. Perhaps he has it made in a backstreet workshop. The Indians are surprisingly adroit at that sort of thing."

"Let's hope the materials they use are up to scratch."

The cockpit door opened and the co-pilot appeared. He shouted something in Hindi and Dua shot to his feet. Bill and Raddick watched him pass between them and stop at the door. After a brief exchange with the co-pilot he chatted on the radio for a few minutes, then spoke to the pilot before returning inside with an ambiguous expression.

"There are new developments, Mr Donaldson."

"What?"

"Your daughter has caught a train to Calcutta. The distance is about the same as Delhi to Varanasi, so she should arrive early this evening."

"Damn. I knew we should have left earlier."

"I think the delay in leaving Delhi has worked to our advantage. I have instructed the pilot to obtain clearance for us to continue to Calcutta. I expect no problem in obtaining it."

"Do we have enough fuel?" Raddick asked.

"Yes, although we will have to climb to a higher altitude and reduce our speed a little." He looked at Bill. "We shall arrive many hours before Sarah, and can meet her at the railway station if you wish."

Bill smiled. "That is good news. What do think, Alan?"

"It might be better if we wait until she's in a hotel before we surprise her. That way she'll be contained in her room with less chance of escape. If we meet her at the station she might panic and run off, or create a scene and cause us problems."

"Why should she run off if we're meeting her with big smiles and open arms?"

"Sometimes big smiles and open arms don't mean jack shit to a schizophrenic, Bill. Sarah may think our very presence is a threat, and any placatory behaviour on our part could be misinterpreted as confirming that." He looked up at Dua. "Was anything said about her behaviour in Varanasi?"

"No," Dua lied.

"What did she do there?" Bill asked.

"What all tourists do - sightseeing."

"Uhm, so how long to Calcutta?"

"No more than two hours."

"Is there anything else I should know?"

"Yes. Your wife arrived in Delhi soon after we took off. She was very agitated due to the late arrival of her flight. However, acting on information from her spies, she has transferred to a Calcutta flight which is due to leave in twenty minutes. I have already instructed my men there to watch her from the moment she arrives."

"Good work, Mr Dua, although the situation does beg some questions. For instance, how did her people know Sarah was in Varanasi and has now left for Calcutta, despite losing her trail in Delhi? If they have been watching her since the kidnap attempt, then why did your people not discover that and inform you so that you could inform me? On the other hand, if my wife's people have not been watching Sarah, then we have the possibility of a security leak."

Dua's expression suggested otherworldly calm as he said, "I can assure you, Mr Donaldson, that there is no security leak. You have employed the best organization in the country for this type of business. It did not get its reputation by impersonating a sieve. However, your wife has employed the second best in the country, although its reputation for using less refined personnel and less than legal methods is well known. To these facts must be added one more. In this country one can hire twenty unemployed people as spies for a day for less than a meal in London, and information on the movements of a foreigner can be obtained for a pittance once word has gone out on the streets. Your wife's agency probably used such methods to pick up your daughter's trail after the kidnap attempt."

"I see. I didn't realize manpower was so cheap. The invoice from your company suggested otherwise."

"The quality of manpower so far used for your particular situation is superior, those engaged having loyalty, intelligence and skills not easily found in a land of poverty and high illiteracy. Therefore, like in your own country, they must be paid accordingly."

"I stand corrected, Mr Dua. Thank you."

"It is my pleasure to assist you, Mr Donaldson." He cleared his throat. "There is one other thing."

"Yes?"

"Your wife is not travelling alone."

"Oh. Who's she with?"

"A young woman called Melissa Burnham, travelling on a British passport."

Raddick stopped breathing in mid-inhalation. Felt suddenly cold. Mentally blank.

Bill looked at him and said, "Things are growing more complicated, Alan."

For a few seconds Raddick stared straight through him with a dark expression that seemed to be cast in stone rather than moulded from flesh. When he refocused on Bill's face he said, "So it seems, but don't ask me why they're travelling together because I haven't got a clue."

"I guess we'll find out in due course, although the fact that you're travelling with me could be reason enough."

"Perhaps," Raddick replied as the past reached out and grabbed him. "Are you going to confront them about why they're here?"

"Not if I can help it. I think it'll be best if we stayed out of their way and just monitored their movements. See who they meet. Incidentally, what's Melissa Burnham's diagnosis?"

"Does there have to be one?"

"In the current circumstances and those relating to the past, I think there has to be one."

Raddick didn't feel like going into details, so kept it superficial. "Personality disordered. Neurotic psychotic. Probably borderline, which has elements of the schizoid, paranoid and obsessive compulsive. Chuck in some free-floating anxiety and depression, a phobia or two and hypochondriasis, plus a fluctuating self-image, impulsivity and an inability to form steady relationships, and you've got a nice little mix with the potential to be lethal. But at the end of the day, who the hell knows for sure? She's never been honest when divulging personal details, and her past is as mysterious as everything else about her. All I can say for sure is that she is a dangerous liar and a surprisingly convincing actress, and she shouldn't be underestimated."

"Just what we need. I suppose Janet had me followed and discovered I was seeing you, and quite by chance found out that Melissa Burnham was spying on you. Probably got her agency people to find out where she lived and then brought her into the equation because she knew you were already in it. It's more likely than Janet simply remembering her from years ago and employing people to find her."

"So Janet goes gunning for you and Melissa goes gunning for me. Maybe they hope to split us up, or at least dilute our combined efforts. But that's overlooking your agency's involvement and potential." He took a deep breath, exhaled slowly and noisily through his mouth in exasperation. "It's all getting a touch crazy. Ha. Melissa Burnham. Here in India. Jesus. There's just no escape from that woman."

"How do you feel about it?"

"To put it bluntly, I'm pissed off. I was hoping the wretched woman had been run over by a bulldozer. Now she's back on my case like a curse that can't be lifted."

Bill waited for more, and when none came, said, "In view of our earlier conversation about Janet's motives, Melissa's presence could be a worry. Does she have psychopathic tendencies?"

"I don't know - maybe."

"Is she capable of killing someone?"

Raddick pursed his lips thoughtfully, brow furrowed. "Probably."

"We could be flying into a lot of trouble, Alan."

"Yeah." You're fucking right there, Bill.

Janet sat with her eyes closed, sweat and stale cuisine clinging to her nose. Beside her Melissa dozed fitfully. Around them the chatter of passengers cut in and out of the engine hum in a constant cycle of peaks and troughs. In the rear a baby began to cry. Somewhere in front an old man coughed up phlegm. Cabin staff moved along the aisle without a smile between them.

Welcome to India, Janet. Yeah, sure, and what a journey it had been to get here, she mused, trying to block off the noise and the pain in her cramped muscles. And it still wasn't over. First, countless hours stuck in one bloody plane, and now another ninety minutes in this soiled can full of tubercular people and itchy seats. If it wasn't for what she had to do, she'd be only too happy to let the sub-continent rot in its own filthy juices.

She cleared her mind of negative thoughts and focused on Calcutta. Her agency contacts there had been primed for action with large amounts of money, even by her standards. A man called Mitra was co-ordinating the team, and would be at the airport to meet her. He was supposedly well-versed in the arts of subterfuge and personnel reduction, the methods utilized dependent on circumstances prevailing at the time unless clients instructed otherwise.

Janet now considered that a heroin overdose was best for Sarah, to ensure a quick death. Sandwiched between the main supply areas of Pakistan and south-east Asia meant there was no shortage of the drug in India. As for Bill and Raddick, Mitra could do what he liked as long as it worked. She stared long and hard at Melissa. Back in England she had seemed useful, but now Mitra was waiting she seemed superfluous. Nevertheless it was worth keeping her close, just in case she was needed to harass and distract Bill and Raddick. There was even an outside chance that her anger could be fuelled to the point where, given a gun, she'd shoot Bill for leading her precious Alan into the swamp of dark depravity. Better still, she might shoot them both, and in turn could be shot herself by one of Mitra's men, who fearing for his life would act in self-defence.

A nice, neat fantasy, but whatever transpired would, she knew, depend on opportunity and circumstance. And anyway, Mitra probably had his own less complicated methods, like a fatal mugging or road accident. Hell, there were more ways to kill than making love, so what was she worrying about? As long as Mitra and his goons didn't lose Sarah or the others, everything would go as smooth as ice. And she'd be there to see it all happen. To know beyond all doubt that it did happen.

Melissa woke to find the man in front of her farting loudly. It smelt of rotten fish and she covered her nose and mouth, glanced at Janet, and assumed she was asleep - had to be asleep: it was the only time the sense of smell didn't work. With a flash of urgency she altered the air-conditioning flow but it made little difference. After a minute the stench dispersed, to be replaced by others less nauseous. God, how she longed to be off this plane and out in the open.

She glanced at Janet again. Whatever the bitch had planned

she was keeping it close. That didn't matter now she'd adjusted to her abrupt self-assertiveness and snap decisions. She could be an opportunist, too, and was, as being in India had proven. Already Hounslow seemed a million miles away, and now Alan was coming ever closer. Soon she would see him, talk to him, point out the error of his ways, and if through his lack of insight and ignorance he rebuffed her again, then she would punish him again. And again and again until he learnt to love her and treated her as his equal.

First, though, she would have to clear the rest of the past from his life, so he could really start afresh. Until Janet turned up she thought she'd cleared that hurdle, but no, there was always some dog foraging around in the bushes of history sniffing out a free meal at someone else's expense. Still, she now had a golden opportunity to sweep away Alan's past once and for all, and build something better for the future.

Once she had overcome his fears and prejudices, his stupidity, arrogance and blindness, he would find her irresistible, and wonder why he had never fallen in love with her sooner. He would yield to her strength, acknowledge her passion, gentleness and courage, and they would laugh about their time in India when they joined forces and swept the mad Donaldsons from the face of the earth.

Sarah gazed out of the window, her thoughts an uneven jigsaw that fogged the passing countryside. Between her mind's eye and the window she formed a nebulous image of Calcutta, with millions of homeless parents roaming like cattle in streets paved with solidified foetuses.

The stench of hopelessness made her sit up with a start. She looked at her fellow passengers through narrowed eyes, wondering which of them was hopeless enough to smell of hopelessness, an odd smell similar to decay, but sweeter, more intimate, like menstrual blood mixed with chop suey and curry powder. After a few seconds she slumped back and relaxed.

It was only a matter of time before she found the nadir of human existence, the shit trail of the spider as it crawled back to her birth and settled in its sticky web, the foetal caul that bridged all parts of her face like the sky bridged poverty, disease and starvation with clouds whose purity was no more than the whiteness of a freshly cleaned urinal.

Jesus, the train ride was boring. If it wasn't for the distinct feeling that she was being followed she would have bought a book or magazine at the station. Now all she had for entertainment were three men intent on dozing, a fat woman doing needlework, a man as thin as a garden rake reading a newspaper full of squiggly lines, and two young kids who kept staring at her. It made travelling on a train in England seem like a flight on Concorde. Oh well, at least she was heading east, into Azad territory, where danger lurked and - fingers crossed - she would find her baby, or at least find out where it was hidden.

She made faces at the kids but got no reaction, and wondered if it was a sign that her own baby was without expression. Without life. The thought depressed her and she stared back out the window. If her baby really was dead she'd find those responsible and kill them. By the blood of Christ she would, and she'd make them hurt just like they'd hurt her when she first became ill. When they'd put more thoughts and ideas into her head than she could handle. Made parts of her body feel alien. Borrowed the odd voices which had occasionally burst around her. Hid the answers to whatever in everyday objects and their positioning, and made the trivial obscurely significant. Fucking bastards.

In the mornings it had been impossible to get out of bed because invisible straps had held her in place. To release them she'd had to hold her breath repeatedly while counting down from fifty to zero, at which point she no longer felt them across her body and could get up to shower in the *en suite* bathroom. Except soap had taken on the texture of sperm and she'd started to make do without it. She'd began to skip breakfast, too, thinking it served no purpose due to its lack of temerity and feminism. After all, what was so daring and sexy about muesli, toast, egg and bacon or suspiciously colourful fruit? The bastards could be strangely alternative.

As for school, she had usually arrived having forgotten a text book or notes, or if she had remembered to do it, her homework. The days had often passed in a blur interspersed with periods of startling clarity. It hadn't been unusual for a lesson to end without her remembering a thing about it, as if walking out the door erased everything that had happened in the classroom. The bastards were powerful.

In the evenings, if not out socializing, she had stayed in her bedroom on the pretext - if one or both of her parents had been at home - of doing her homework. More often than not she had filled notebooks with poetry, most of it incomprehensible; or had listened to her walkman as it delivered the wisdom of star music and cosmic thoughts from an empty cassette chamber; or had watched television and siphoned off messages other than those intended; or had played CDs of her favourite music, catching the signs that had encouraged her to cut loose. When she moved around her bedroom she had followed red guidelines on the carpet, and when she touched furniture, books or electrical appliances she had done so in a certain way, as though performing a brief autistic ritual.

Yet despite the intrusive nature of her dysfunction, she had been capable of appearing and sounding normal for hours at a stretch. The only thing she had sensed wrong at the time had been the behaviour towards her of the people she had mixed with. At times they hadn't seemed themselves at all.

Sarah grimaced. Despite the evidence she'd been coerced into leaving around by the bastards, no one really knew a tenth of it all. They were all showroom dummies from a

Kraftwerk factory. Ask a question and the mannequins would fart meaninglessly through their mouths, robots expelling trash fumes, expecting others to recycle their garbage. Well, not any more. She was going to recycle them, just as Mother Nature had once recycled her.

It had happened numerous tree rings ago. She presented herself on the doorstep and rang and rang and rang that fucking doorbell until she was sprouting roots. Mummy killer cow finally ordained to answer the door, and gasped as Sarah slouched in, her dress soaked through and as earth-stained as her face, hands, legs and feet. She stood shivering on the door mat, bits of dead leaf and twig in her hair, and leaned to one side as her mother closed the door and looked her up and down with disgust and utter disbelief.

After that nothing much happened for a while. Janet lost her expression, as though such an unorthodox entry had suddenly become entirely expected, wholly appropriate to the circumstances, a constant unchangeable confirmation of mental illness, like a nose, mouth and eyes confirming the existence of a face, and therefore not worthy of any particular reaction.

A moment later all that changed unexpectedly as her mother hugged her tightly. She had never done that before, when Sarah had been neat and clean, so why do it now when she was dirty and wet? Sarah looked over her shoulder and saw her father and an uncle and aunt. So that was it. Mummy killer cow was performing! It didn't make sense otherwise.

Sarah screwed the act with one of her own.

"I fucked the forest," she stated matter-of-factly. "Gave love to Mother Earth in rain to feel her muddy kiss on your cold skin. The winter sog of leafy hair is the wet stroke of grassy fur on the rough bark of her lungs. The pain is giving as trees fuck and fill the mouth with star shit. You can't scream till covered with earth of earth and Mother Earth empty cold of night hisses. You craved that of all people craved that."

Her voice grew louder. "You hear the call of forest, the shriek of mother bastards rape her over over, fill her with poisonous sperm as they rip babies from her gut and burn them in furnace fires and fucking motor cars and spread their ashes in the fucking sky. Either of you."

Janet and Bill looked dumbstruck, both lost for words. The uncle and aunt retreated with ashen faces from behind which fear manufactured hairline cracks and ejected beads of fear juice. Yes, to recycle is to live again. Not so much reincarnation, as a progression, like an egg to a caterpillar to a chrysalis to a butterfly.

12

GATHERING

Bill, Raddick and Dua went by taxi from the airport to the Grand Lindsay Hotel on busy Nehru Road, in the centre of Calcutta. The journey took two hours due to congestion, roadworks and broken down vehicles, and exhaust fumes seeped into the car at regular intervals.

Once Dua had escorted them to their rooms, he left to check with his team on the latest developments, promising to return in the evening to take them to dinner. Within minutes of his departure, Bill found himself staring unseeing out of the window, wondering why he considered himself so normal while those around him seemed so abnormal.

Perhaps he was simply lucky: no obviously wayward genes in the family tree, no traumatic childhood or teens, only loving, supportive parents and two affectionate sisters, plus the benefits of an intelligently interactive middle-class household and friends from a similar background. He was tempted to think that his developmental circumstances were not too different from Sarah's, but they were. He and Janet had not been as supportive, close or loving as his own parents had been toward him. Plenty of lip service and encouragement but no in-depth interest; always too busy with work, doing things the modern way. And Sarah had no siblings, only a variety of nannies and friends who came and went. Maybe she had been too alone for someone with her genetic disposition - and where had that come from? It had to be Janet's side. Was that why she had spoken so infrequently about her family? If he had to draw her family tree it would be a stump. Her parents apparently died in her teens, mother from cancer, father from a stroke. She had a brother she hadn't seen for years because of some disagreement. She may have mentioned aunts, uncles and cousins, but if so it had been so rarely he couldn't recall anything she'd said about them. It all suggested secrets - unhappiness, unsavoury deeds, mental illness - who knew what?

When he first met Janet it had been at university. She was dark and a bit wild, very sexy. He had been a bit of a lad himself back then, stretching his wings in a new form of freedom. Quite why they had hit it off he never knew, but they had, and that seemed enough at the time. The sex had been good, they'd got drunk together over the weekends, and on occasion had even studied together, helping each other. Their relationship had been well-balanced: uninhibited at times, sensible other times, with enough space for both of them to exercise their own independence, and Janet insisted on that, as though without it she couldn't survive. Looking back he realized just how secretive she had always been, yet he had never noticed it at the time. Was that because she could talk about a million things except herself and her feelings?

Janet had been his first proper girlfriend, and he hadn't strayed once in his life. Only grown distant, a nagging discontent occasionally pulling at his heart strings, like a mid-life crisis. What was it Sarah had once said to him? You look like a cross between the actors Bill Patterson and Bob Peck. He'd never heard of them and she had shown him their photographs in a magazine. He had been rather shocked. He always imagined himself as.......what? He wasn't sure, but certainly different from how Sarah had seen him.

A sudden wave of combined anger and sadness swept up in him. He turned from the window and cut off his thoughts. Raddick. He'd better go and see him. He strolled down the corridor to Raddick's room and knocked. Raddick let him in.

"Dinner at nine with Dua. I bet you a rupee he doesn't pay for it." Bill looked around. "Your room is the same as mine,

124

not bad but not particularly good. At least we're not in the front of the building, otherwise the noise would keep us awake."

Raddick yawned. "At least it's better than my bedsit."

"Tired?"

"Yes."

"I suggest you get some sleep. I'll buzz you through about eight. Dua should have some news for us when he comes, then we can decide what to do about Sarah."

"You plan to see her tonight, if possible?"

"No. Tomorrow would be better - unless Janet queers the pitch."

Mitra met Janet and Melissa at Dum Dum Airport. He was tall, ruggedly handsome, about forty, and dressed in well-tailored casuals. He gave them a brief history lesson as they walked to his car.

"The airport stands on the site of the old British army Dum-Dum Arsenal, where the dum-dum bullet was invented in eighteen ninety-eight. It was originally a soft-nosed point three-o-three rifle bullet, but the term is now applied to any bullet with a soft nose."

Janet's response was as sour as her mood. "How very interesting."

Mitra laughed. "But it is, Mrs Donaldson. It's a man-stopper in the truest sense. You see, when the bullet hits the target it expands and lacerates in a most horrible fashion, which is no doubt why such bullets were banned by the Hague Convention a year later."

"That's a shame," Janet said, glancing at him out the corner of her eye. He was smiling at her, and she was beginning to get his drift. "Do they still exist?"

"Not officially."

"But unofficially?"

"I think some can still be found," and his smile widened.

"I think dum-dum is a very dumb name," Melissa shrilled.

Janet forced a laugh. "Isn't it just," and then in a whisper only Melissa could hear, "but it was a man who invented it so perhaps it's really quite appropriate."

Melissa's laugh was more like the screech of a gull, and Janet wished she hadn't said anything.

"A joke?" enquired Mitra.

"Humour her," whispered Janet.

In Mitra's Mercedes Janet allowed her thoughts to eddy around the notion of using dum-dums to despatch Bill, Raddick and the wretched herring gull sitting next to her. But not Sarah. Her demise had to be swift and bloodless.

"What hotel are we staying at?" she asked, suddenly bored with her day-dreaming.

"The Maidan Royale on Nehru Road in the centre of the city. It is very nice, and I have booked a double room for each of you." He glanced at her in his rear-view mirror.

"Nice car. Why haven't you got one like all the others?" She looked out the window. "They look so old fashioned I'm tempted to think the British left them behind."

"They left the blueprints, Mrs Donaldson, and we have been making them ever since because of import restrictions. However, these have been considerably relaxed and we now see many more western cars on our streets. This one was purchased from an embassy in Delhi."

"What about another western car, with two Englishmen in it?"

"The car you have in mind was, in fact, a taxi. They were with their agency man, a fellow called Dua." He told her what hotel they had checked into. "I have them under surveillance."

"And my daughter?"

"Her train is due to arrive this evening. With luck she will head straight for the cheap backpackers' area off Nehru Road, so everyone you are interested in will be very close. This advantage allows us to increase our efficiency in the areas of surveillance, communications and rapid deployment. However, I must ask you both not to go walking in the area - or any other - without first checking with me, in case you accidentally meet one of the opposition. Also, if you do go out I will provide you with an escort, just to keep beggars away you understand, otherwise they can be quite bothersome."

"I've no doubt." Janet didn't plan to walk far anywhere in this filthy teeming hell-hole. It was far too ugly.

"I can see one now," Melissa pointed out. "Look, over there."

Janet indulged her. "Oh yes, the woman with the child."

"He's only got one arm."

"Maybe the other fell off."

Mitra chuckled. "Our leprosy problems are no longer that bad. Most likely his arm was cut off. It is normal for beggar-caste parents to chop off their child's arm or leg to increase sympathy for them from strangers, who wishing for good karma will then donate more than they otherwise would."

"That's absolutely barbarous," Melissa protested. "How can such things be allowed to happen?"

"It is the way of a million lifetimes. You cannot stop overnight something which has endured for centuries. One day, though, it will stop, and already it happens less and less."

"When can I talk to you about the situation that brings me here?" Janet asked, not interested in hearing more.

"Tonight, over dinner?"

"How about when we get to the hotel?"

"As you wish."

"What about me?" Melissa asked Janet testily. "I'm part of your plan, too, you know."

"I've got to discuss finances with Mr Mitra, which is why I want to talk to him in private."

"So when are we going to make our plans?"

"After Sarah has arrived - tomorrow, after we've caught up on our sleep and sat in the bath for an hour or two." She squeezed Melissa's hand. It felt like a wet rag and she quickly released it. "Then with Mr Mitra's help we can sort out our problems once and for all."

Melissa gazed out the window, wishing she could be outside, yet at the same time frightened by the differences between the people and herself. Despite being considerably more downtrodden than their counterparts in Hounslow, their eyes were more intense - fiercer, as if a terrible hatred lurked within them, waiting for any excuse that would unleash it via knives and fists or whatever was to hand.

It was a hatred she recognized, had harboured for most of her life. She kept it hidden in her heart, away from the soul and mind which the eyes constantly betrayed. So far she had used only tiny amounts of it, but knew that the day was fast approaching when the ideal excuse to unleash it would present itself. And when it did, the violence would be extreme.

With that thought in mind she glanced slyly at Janet, and hoped the day would come soon. Very soon.

13

THUNDER

Dua took Bill and Raddick to a restaurant in nearby Park Street. The furnishings were luxurious, the service deferential, the food reputed to be excellent. A minute after they arrived Mitra slipped in the back way and struck a costly deal with the manager, who took care of their order personally.

Raddick had chosen a lamb curry, and as the chef prepared it, Mitra slipped him two thousand rupees and added an ingredient of his own. It was a potion similar to hyoscine that combined with the bottle of wine the three had ordered, would begin to produce a mildly disorientating and euphoric high within ninety minutes. By the second hour Raddick would feel slightly drunk, but more importantly, would lose his ability to discriminate and make reasoned judgements.

When the food arrived it looked impressive, and the three ate with undisguised zeal, Raddick the first to clear his plate. With a flush of satisfaction he poured himself another glass of wine and sat back with a contented smile.

The manager went into the kitchen to make his final report. Mitra slapped the chef on the back and left by the back door. Three of his men took up their positions outside the restaurant. Everybody relaxed.

"So what are we going to do about Sarah?" Raddick asked. "Pay her a visit early tomorrow morning?"

"I think that's best," Bill replied, "and if necessary we can transfer her to the apartment Mr Dua has kindly offered us."

"It is best, I think," Dua pushed, angling for more fees. "You will be able to keep a closer eye on her there."

"What's the place like where she's staying?"

"It is a typical low-budget hotel full of backpackers. The staff are young and amenable. We can expect no problems with them."

"What time is best for us to move in with minimum disturbance?"

Dua looked thoughtful for a moment, his beady eyes searching for crumbs on the tablecloth. He found one and rolled it about with an index finger. "Six o'clock," he said. "The staff will probably be up but most of the travellers will still be asleep."

"And if my wife plans something similar for the same time?"

"If such action should look probable, she will find numerous obstacles in her path that will slow her down considerably. By the time she gets to Sarah's hotel we will have executed our plan and be long gone."

"In view of how close Janet and Melissa's hotel is, I'm damned glad they didn't come here for a meal," Raddick said light-heartedly.

"I would know in advance," Dua said confidently.

"Okay," said Bill. "We'd better finish off here and get back for some sleep. Tomorrow could be a very long day."

Raddick raised his glass. "To a successful mission," and he finished the wine in one gulp.

Janet paced her room waiting for Mitra. If he didn't succeed with stage one of their plan, they'd have to think of something else. What she needed was a gin and tonic. Bloody place didn't even have drinks in the rooms. Damned city. Even at the back of the hotel she could hear the hum of traffic. Taste air tainted with poison. Catch the odd cry from some disease-ridden inhabitant. Jesus, was all this worth two million or more? She smiled sharply. Of course it was.

There was a knock on the door. She opened it, saw Mitra, let him in. He was smiling.

"Successful?"

"Yes."

"That's a relief. Are the girls ready?"

"Two of them, the most beautiful the city has to offer."

Janet didn't dare think what beautiful meant in Calcutta.

"How long have we got?"

"It starts at midnight."

Janet checked her watch. "An hour to go. The shrew is asleep in her room. Do you fancy a quick drink downstairs? I'm gasping for one."

"It would be my pleasure. I'll just summon one of my men to keep an eye on the corridor, in case our friend wakes up and wanders off."

He pulled out a radio, fired off a salvo of words and stuck it back in his pocket.

"That looks very small and hi-tech for India," Janet observed.

"It is. I like to use my own imported equipment. It makes life easier. Shall we go?"

Raddick walked unsteadily to his hotel room, Bill at his side.

"You alright, Alan?"

"Feel a bit weird."

"Uhm, I hope you're not coming down with anything."

Raddick stopped by his door, unlocked it, said, "Strong wine. Not used to it since prison."

"You get a good night's sleep. Dua's waking us at five."

"Okay, and thanks for the meal. It really was excellent."

"Told you Dua wouldn't pay for it. See you tomorrow."

"Goodnight."

Raddick entered his room, closed the door, switched on the light and fell on his bed. He wanted to sleep as he was, face down with his clothes on, but couldn't, and turned over to stare at the ceiling.

India. He could hardly believe he was here. And all thanks

131

to Bill. What a nice man. And tomorrow he'd see Sarah. Nice kid. Sad. Helping her would make him feel good. And she deserved his help. She wasn't bad looking, either. Was the ceiling moving? Surely he wasn't drunk? Maybe he was, but what did it matter? He was in Calcutta!

Janet paced her room, waiting for Mitra to phone. The dirty dog had placed a hand on her arm in the bar. What did he think she was? She checked the time. Midnight already. All this hanging around was driving her mad. The drink in the bar hadn't helped. Just made her want another and another. Bloody Sarah. Why hadn't she picked Europe or America? Fucking typical of her, illness or no illness. And now she was in some shithole round the corner with a bunch of scruffy sods who thought travelling through Asia with sixty-pound packs on their backs was a necessary experience. Bloody fools. No wonder the world was turning to shit when idiots like that represented the future.

The phone rang. She snatched it up. Listened. Said a few words and replaced the receiver. It was time to kick the shrew.

She walked to Melissa's room, let herself in with a duplicate key, found her curled fully-clothed in a foetal position on the bed. She shook her roughly and told her to get up.

Melissa sat up sluggishly, rubbed the sleep from her eyes.

"What's happening?"

"Alan's gone off the rails."

"What? How?"

"I don't know, but we've got to see him, save him, whatever. Come on, pull yourself together. We haven't got much time."

"I'm ready," Melissa said, jumping up.

"Good, let's go," and she opened the door and hurried out.

In reception they were met by one of Mitra's men and escorted to the Grand Lindsay Hotel, a few minutes walk away. The air was cool and smelt of hydrocarbon. Clouds blotted the sky. Traffic was thin, pedestrians sparse. Dark doorways coughed in their sleep.

They entered the hotel by a fire exit already opened from inside by another of Mitra's men. When they got to Raddick's room on the third floor they heard girlish laughter coming from inside. Melissa put an ear to the door and listened. What she heard drew a veil of fury over her face.

Janet bit her tongue to prevent herself from laughing. The shrew had become an angry rat with a twitching nose and quivering lips. Poor Melissa. Now all she had to do was open the door and vent her rage at being betrayed.

"What's happening inside?" she asked in a whisper.

Melissa stepped back, trembling noticeably, and stared at the door. "He's got girls in there with him." Her hands balled into fists, but she made no attempt to knock on the door or open it.

"Must be prostitutes," Janet said, "in which case we'd better stop him before he gets syphilis or worse. Try the door, it might be unlocked."

Melissa turned the handle, opened the door a little, peeped in. Raddick was naked on the bed, laughing heartily as two naked girls no older than sixteen rubbed themselves against his body. With an angry intake of breath she barged in and shouted, "What the hell do you think you're playing at, you filthy bastard?"

The girls slid off, revealing an erect penis, and grabbing their saris fled into the bathroom without a trace of shock on their faces. Janet was surprised by how attractive they were. In comparison Melissa was simply a malformation. She looked at her standing at the foot of the bed, her fists opening and closing as Raddick continued laughing. For Christ's sake do something, she thought, glancing at Mitra's man who merely shrugged and closed the door.

"Alan!" The word shot out like a cannonade. "Alan, you

bastard."

Raddick's laughter died down as he finally realized who she was. He sat up chuckling, and made no effort to cover his nakedness.

"Melissa dar-ling, how nice to see you. Have you come to join the orgy? To taste the black holes of Calcutta?" and he roared with laughter at his little joke.

Melissa moved to the side of the bed, her gaze as hard as diamond, fists so tight her knuckles were white. "How could you?" she yelled. "How could you stoop so low?" And she punched him in the face.

He stopped laughing and rubbed his cheek. "What did you do that for?" he said, so softly that with his perplexed expression it almost made Janet laugh.

"You know why?" and she hit him again.

This time he frowned, looked at Janet and said, "You here too?"

The girls shot out of the bathroom and dashed to the door.

"Where you going?" Raddick cried.

"You filthy fucking whores," Melissa shouted as they disappeared into the corridor, Mitra's man closing the door behind them.

"Me-lis-sa, why you so angry with them? Is it because they're so beautiful and you're so ugly?"

"Cover yourself," she ordered.

Raddick fingered his penis. "Why? Don't you like it?"

Melissa's face turned a darker shade of red. Janet wondered if she was going to stand there all night. Before she could say anything Raddick invited her to sample his body.

"Come on Janet, a good fuck would do you good. Unlike Melissa here. She needs an enema. A good gallon of mustard."

It was the trigger Janet had been waiting for. As Raddick hooted with laughter, Melissa attacked him with a screaming vengeance, her fists pounding his face. Mitra's man closed in, gestured for Janet to move back to the door, and pulled out a

134

knife.

Janet moved quickly, looked back as Raddick finally defended himself by grabbing Melissa's arms, forcing her over his chest. She wriggled sideways, kneed him twice in the balls. He groaned, twisted, let go of one arm and instinctively shielded his genitals with his free hand. She punched him in the mouth, bit his arm, tried to roll off the bed. Grabbing her hips he dragged her back, got an elbow in the face. Furious, he yanked her head round by her hair and slapped her face before throwing her face-down on the bed.

"Fucking lunatic chasing me across the world, destroying everything I've got." He sat on her legs, tugged at the back of her slacks. "You ruined everything you fucking lunatic."

Melissa struggled forward until her head was over the edge of the bed and the waistband of her slacks was halfway down her buttocks.

Mitra's man seized his moment, gestured for Janet to switch off the light. She did so, heard Melissa squeak, Raddick curse, then switched it back on. The knife laid on the carpet between Melissa's hands.

Raddick carried on tugging, oblivious of the knife, the fingers curling around its handle. When he finally had Melissa's buttocks fully exposed her response was so swift that the blade sliced twice before he felt the pain or the others realized what she'd done. Before anyone could react she slashed twice more, catching Raddick across the chest. He sprung off her to the floor, eyes wide as she lunged after him.

Mitra's man opened the door, pulled Janet out as the knife swept down towards Raddick's face. Then he closed the door and she saw only wood, a muffled cry coming from behind it. Suddenly aware of how much noise there must have been, she glanced anxiously up and down the corridor, expecting to see people looking out. There was only another of Mitra's men waiting by the fire exit, his hand flicking urgently.

Janet grinned all the way back to her hotel, where Mitra

met her in the bar. At a secluded corner table she told him what had happened.

"I really had doubts at one time whether it would work, but it turned out beautifully. The poor creature was quite beside herself with humiliation and rage."

"I am pleased that you are happy."

"Thank you. Your idea about her wounding him rather than killing him was sensible, although he might end up dead, she was so angry."

"It is doubtful she could kill someone like him with a knife, unless she stabbed him deeply in a vulnerable area."

"If she has it doesn't really matter."

"No, but as I told you, it is best to kill only when one has to. Your objective was to remove him from the scene. This I could have done without Melissa."

"I know, but as I made the mistake of bringing her here, I thought we might as well make use of her - and get rid of her at the same time. With luck Raddick will end up in hospital and she'll end up in some stinking prison."

Low static sounded from Mitra's pocket. He took out his radio and spoke into it. Someone spoke back. He replaced it in his pocket.

"It seems the police and an ambulance have been called to your husband's hotel. A man was seriously wounded by his girlfriend in a knife attack. She, alas, seems to have disappeared."

"You mean she's escaped?"

Mitra nodded. "But do not worry. My men or the police will find her, and when they do, you've been out all night with me, with no idea where she was or what she was doing." He smiled suggestively. "And then, in a few hours time, we can visit your daughter."

"Mr Mitra, you're a gentleman." A greasy stupid one.

The commotion of officialdom woke Bill and most of the

guests on his floor. When he looked out and saw policemen standing outside Raddick's room, he quickly dressed and went out to investigate. Dua had already beaten him to it, and intercepted him. Back in his room, Bill demanded to know what had happened.

"Your friend was attacked by the woman travelling with your wife. Unfortunately she has escaped, but I have arranged for Mr Raddick to be taken to a private hospital. He is on his way there now, and his injuries are not serious. He was still moving around and talking."

It took several seconds for Bill to absorb the information.

"I'm paying you for protection in addition to everything else. What the hell happened?"

"It appears that Mr Raddick was entertaining two prostitutes when this woman burst in and attacked him with a knife."

"Prostitutes? Where did he get them? I saw him into his room as soon as we returned from the restaurant, and they weren't with him them. Jesus, he was barely able to walk in a straight line, let alone go looking for whores."

"He told me they knocked on his door and simply walked in. I suspect they were sent as part of a plan. I also suspect that he was drugged in the restaurant with a concoction that made him soft and susceptible to suggestion. He was somewhat confused when I spoke to him, but the little he said seems to confirm this, as did his eyes. The pupils were very large and he had a glassy stare."

"What did he say about Melissa Burnham - why she attacked him?"

"Not much, but he did say that your wife and a man - probably one of her agency thugs - were also present, but didn't stay. I've told him not to mention this to the police, at least not for the time being, otherwise they may wish to ask you awkward questions."

"Why didn't you wake me as soon as you got here?"

"I didn't want policemen asking you questions before I found out what had happened. It is best you keep low for the moment. They may want to speak to you later, but later can be delayed until you are back in England. As for your friend, they won't trouble him for another day or so, longer if the hospital exaggerates his condition."

"Where's my wife now?"

"In her hotel room."

"And Sarah?"

"As before, quite safe. I have, though, taken the precaution of increasing the number of men watching her, so if your wife tries anything she can be adequately protected."

"In the circumstances that's the least you can do. As for now, I want you to take me to Alan."

"Of course. I have a car waiting."

Raddick's wounds were numerous, but mainly superficial. He had cut lips, facial bruising, and a couple of knife nicks on his cheek. Across his chest were two long slashes, not quite deep enough to need stitches, and a third line cut across them from his neck. On his arms were deeper gashes, some stitched, and his thighs and stomach held other, less serious wounds.

"I thought she was going to castrate me," he told Bill. "I'm lucky she didn't, because she could have done, easy. I wasn't with it at all. Felt like being in some weird dream, everything slow, slightly out of focus. Guess I'm lucky to be alive considering who did it." He shook his head. "She's a fucking nightmare, a shadow I can't get rid of. Who'd have thought she'd turn up in my hotel room with a bloody knife?"

"That's Janet for you. What's it like here?"

"National Health Service, early sixties." He pushed himself more upright, hands clasped in his lap. "Things are getting messy, Bill. What are we going to do? Pay Sarah a visit as planned?"

"If we don't get some sleep we're going to be fit for nothing, but I feel time is running out. I don't know. Are you up to it?"

"I'm too pissed off to sleep. As long as I don't play rugby I should be okay. They've given me some pain killers."

"I don't feel like sleeping, either. Perhaps we should go back to the hotel and freshen up, then do what we've planned."

Raddick swung his feet off the bed. "Okay, let's do it."

14

CUTTING LOOSE

A dark green room squeezed Sarah tight. Dawn light magnified dust motes. From outside came hammering. Each blow skewered her ears, reverberated in her skull, threatened to wake her voices. She looked around the room. It was unfamiliar.

The hammering ceased.

Silence spawned memories of a train journey that seemed to last forever: a steam train from Varanasi, its carriage windows barred like an asylum express carrying lunatics to an even greater madness.

Calcutta. Was she here already? The confusion of Howrah station droned pictureless in her mind. Crossing the monstrously ugly and insanely busy Howrah Bridge came back to haunt her. She reached out, snatched a city map from a bedside chair, unfolded it and homed in on a large patch of green - the Maidan, a park in the Chowringhee district that bordered the east side of the Hooghly River. Next to the Maidan, Sudder Street had been circled in black biro. Off it, too small for the map, was Stuart Lane, where she had found the Paragon Hotel. Her finger wandered over the map for ten minutes before she found what she was looking for.

Kali's house.

It was time to visit her sister.

After washing in the communal facilities and going to the toilet, she returned to her room, strapped on her money belt, locked her door and set off down the corridor. As soon as she turned into the dining area which led to reception, she froze, hardly able to believe what she saw. At the far end stood

Raddick and her father with a short Indian man, talking to a sleepy member of staff. Fearful of their intentions, she stepped back round the corner, then peeped out. They were coming her way.

Galvanized with panic she looked around for a hiding place, and darted into a toilet cubicle. Holding her breath she waited, heard them walk past. When their footsteps grew distant she looked out, saw no one, but heard rapping on a door. Guessing it was her door, she decided it was now or never.

She slipped out, walking carefully lest the concrete floors made her sneakers squeak, and got as far as reception before she heard a shout behind her. Without looking back she crashed open the door and bolted into the lane, straight into the arms of a man.

Without thinking she headbutted him, stuck her thumbs in his eyes. He screamed, let go, and she ran, another man rushing from a doorway and grabbing her arm. She tried to pull free, swung her fist, missed, and kicked him in the shin. He held on, cursing, and she kicked him again. His grip tightened as he twisted her arm, moved sideways, hooked her round the neck.

Raddick and Bill appeared, shouted her name, ran towards her. She writhed desperately, managed to sink her teeth into the man's arm and jerking her head back, crack his nose. With an anguished cry he released her, but before she could run another man, bigger than the others, locked his arms around her and squeezed hard. The air shot out of her in a long groan, then her father materialized before her.

"Let her go," he ordered. "You're hurting her."

Sarah shook herself free, glared at him and shouted, "Stay away you thieving bastard, I know you stole my baby." She struck him in the face and sprinted off towards Sudder Street.

The blow and accusation stunned Bill, and as Dua fired off commands and his men gave chase, he stood dumbly, curious street dwellers woken by the fracas moving closer.

Raddick came alongside, asked if he was okay. When Bill didn't reply he stared uncertainly at him and said, "What did she mean about the baby?"

"You tell me, you're the psychiatrist."

There was fear in his eyes, and Raddick knew he was hiding something. "Has she ever been pregnant?"

Bill shot him a disdainful look, said, "Come on, let's catch them up," and trotted off.

Raddick made no attempt to follow him until Dua said, "He has paid us to help him, so let us do so."

Sarah ran up Sudder Street like a greyhound, Nehru Road beckoning with light traffic. As she reached it a car swung round the corner and braked sharply. She careered into it, sprawled across a front wing, landed on a pile of builders' rubble. Furious, she leapt to her feet and saw her mother staring incredulously at her from the back seat.

Oh God, she thought, staring back, they were all out to get her today - demons, witches, warlocks and all. When her mother lowered the window and Mitra and one of his men got out, she picked up a chuck of masonry and glanced back at Dua's men running towards her.

Janet stuck her head out, called Sarah's name. Mitra uttered what he thought were soothing words. His man moved in close, eyeing her carefully, and stopped within touching distance.

"Please put stone down," he said softly. "No one will hurt you."

Sarah slammed it into his face then hurled it at Mitra, grabbed her mother by the hair and shouted, "Where's my baby you fucking bitch? What have you done with it?"

One of Dua's men reached the car, grabbed her round the waist. As he pulled her away, a handful of Janet's hair coming with her, he lost his footing on the rubble and fell flat on his

142

back, Sarah on top of him, twisting, facing him, a brick in her hand which plunged into his face. Then she was gone, the rest of Dua's men in pursuit.

As Bill and Raddick reached the scene and stopped, followed by Dua who continued on, Janet got out the car, a hurricane about to discharge its wrath. Before she could utter a word Melissa appeared from nowhere and laid her out with an iron bar, then ran off. For Bill it was virtually the last straw, and he slumped against a wall, lost in the mounting chaos.

Raddick inspected the wounded, not knowing who to attend to first. A silent crowd gathered around them. Mitra pulled himself up, blood trickling down the side of his face. His radio crackled in his pocket. He took it out, spoke, listened, and finally looked across at Bill with a hostile expression.

"They lost her in the underground station. She jumped on a train before they could stop her. Perhaps it's time you considered using professionals."

Bill glanced at Janet, unconscious on the ground. "Tell that to my wife," he replied bitterly.

Sarah left Calcutta's short solitary underground line at Kalighat, three miles south of Chowringhee. Within ten minutes she was hiding behind a wall, frightened and tired, and in no doubt that her baby was close. She smoked three cigarettes and an hour later fell asleep.

She woke with the sun on her face, and by midday was standing outside the Kali Temple complex, watching people swarm in and out. The smell of fresh blood permeated the hot, dusty air.

And her voices stirred as she entered.

Cream, yellow and grey walls embraced her. Green slats hung over narrow archways like rotting half-eaten eyelids. People swirled around her, chatting incomprehensibly.

Sunshine illuminated walls; deep shadow hid others. The blood-smell moved thickly through the light and dark.

Sarah tasted it.

Heard it.

Smiled.

She moved slowly, hunting out the thicker densities of the sweet metallic scent. They led her to the ritual beheading of goats and young water buffalo, and narrowed her eyes as hot red spattered dusty concrete, collected in shimmering pools, played host to innumerable flies. Her gruff voice woke from its slumber.

"Typical of you to come here in an effort to hide the stench of your menstruation."

"I'm not menstruating," she whispered.

"You're always menstruating, you filthy bitch."

A headless goat fell to its knees, blood spurting from its thin white neck.

Sarah spun round. Kali had helped her in Varanasi, now where the hell was she with her signs? She wanted her baby or the stinking bastard fathers who had deserted her. She wanted them screaming as she tore off their polluting testicles. Instead she had headless fucking livestock.

She scanned the entranceways into the temple and outbuildings, shivered as the blackness within them poured out and dispersed into invisibility. She turned back as a buffalo calf squealed, its eyes impossibly wide with the terror of the sword, and gagged as the temple wrapped her in death and fear, human sweat and body heat, the blood, shit and piss of animals.

Revolted by the sacrificial enclosure, she pushed through the crowds that had grown behind her and sought a way out of the complex.

Depressed and angry, her head a mass of conflicting thoughts, she tripped over the legs of a scruffy man sitting by the exit. He jumped up as she fell, apologized profusely in an unexpected English accent, and helped her up. In a surge of intense anger she raised her hand to strike him, but stopped short when she saw his eyes. They were sadder than any she had ever seen.

She stepped back for a better look at him and wished she hadn't. His dark brown face was dotted with boils. She looked at his eyes again. Yes, they were as sad as she had thought, but the sadness, she now saw, hid their small pigginess. And his skull was domed and his head too large for his skinny frame.

"I am Swami Vivekananda," he said, "a messenger from the great temple in the sky. I have a degree in English Language, but alas, India is a hard place for educated fellows who have been abandoned by their family, friends and work colleagues. Why are you here?"

"I came for a sign from Kali, but she let me down. I'm looking for my baby. It's been stolen."

"Stolen!" and he lifted his hands in horror. "How terrible. When did this happen? You must inform the police immediately."

"No need. It was stolen in England, along with everything else. They stole everything from me except my soul, the bastards."

Swami nodded. "I understand perfectly. My soul is all I have. Look at how they left me." He turned slightly, revealing a hump.

Sarah looked up at the pure blue sky and sucked it in. "Why are they killing animals in there? It's like a butcher's carnival."

"It is Kali's birthday. They cook the meat and give it to the poor. That is why I am here."

"Kali's birthday is in January. I looked it up."

"She has many birthdays, depending on which of her manifestations is being celebrated."

"I thought she was my friend," Sarah said despondently.

"She is," Swami confirmed. "You said she let you down, but I do not think she would on her birthday, do you? Perhaps the sign you are looking for will come later, at a time Kali thinks more appropriate. Besides, when she died and her corpse was cut into pieces, one of her fingers fell on this spot, which then became a place of Hindu worship. Therefore Kali Temple today is doubly favourable for you."

Sarah smiled. "That's nice. Do you think a river might help? Rivers are salvation, you know. I think I must go to the Hooghly."

"A wise choice. It is special to Kali."

"Really?" Her smile broadened, softening her features. "Let's go then. I'll pay for everything. Are you hungry? We can eat on the way. Come on," and she started walking, gesturing for him to follow.

"Another acquisition, you stupid cow," said the gruff voice.

And the shrill voice added, "The world is her oyster and she has found a pearl. Life is an acquisition."

"Life's a fucking inquisition, you shrill little shit, and there'll be boogly in the fucking Hooghly when Kali comes to parley, you mark my words. The stupid little slut is always getting into trouble."

Sarah pleaded silently with the gruff voice not to spoil her good mood. Suspiciously, it obeyed without protest.

15

KISSING THE RAZOR'S EDGE

"Your wife has a large bump on her head and a headache," Dua informed Bill as they sat in the Grand Lindsay bar. "Her x-ray at the hospital showed no structural damage. She is currently recuperating in her room, and is apparently in a most foul mood."

"Good."

"Maybe, but it could make her even more troublesome. Already this Mitra who is helping her has men everywhere looking for Sarah - as indeed do I - and I have found out that he has a most unpleasant reputation."

"How so?"

"He has been linked with all manner of crimes, including murder. I have heard it said that he occasionally undertakes assassinations."

"Just what I need."

"I do not think he is involved in this matter to try anything of that nature, otherwise he would have already struck without revealing himself."

Bill scanned the bar anxiously. "Maybe there are others. You don't know my wife."

Dua frowned. "Are you saying that she wishes to harm you and your daughter?"

"Sarah's her daughter, too, and I'm sure she engineered the attack on Alan."

"Yes, of course, but I remain puzzled about your wife's true intentions. You have never made this clear to me."

"My wife is unbalanced. I don't know what she's up to."

"You must have suspicions, Mr Donaldson."

"All I know is that I want to leave India with Sarah as soon as possible." He took a sip of his scotch. "Is there any news on her?"

"A little. She has been seen walking in various areas near here, in the company of a somewhat deformed man - a beggar type."

Bill sighed. "Where are they going? What are they doing?"

"Reports suggest that they are heading towards Howrah, but as we are following their trail it is hard to say what their intentions are. As for their activities, it is simply walking and talking. I expect to find their exact whereabouts very soon."

"Any news on Melissa Burnham?"

"No."

"Where's Alan?"

"Asleep in his room."

"That's what I intend to do." He finished his scotch. "It'll be night soon. I would like Sarah found before then. Is the Lear Jet still at the airport?"

"Yes, with maximum fuel. The crew are on stand-by."

"Good." He stood up. "Wake me as soon as you have some definite news. I want to be present when we take her. And please, try to ensure that this time it doesn't turn into a running battle."

"I will do my best, Mr Donaldson, but please bear in mind that your daughter is not the easiest person to apprehend. Also, we have to consider Mitra and his men. If they try and stop us matters could become most awkward."

"That's one of the problems I'm paying you to deal with, Mr Dua, so I suggest you give it some thought."

Dua scowled at his back as he walked off.

Filthy squat-hole sediment. Bacteria infested slums and slime. Hidden beggars rutting in the flesh of moist sewage. Sarah sensed it all, yawned, looked up and down the alley they were in. It tapered to invisibility at both ends, dark and silent. On each side, ready to fall, stood decaying buildings of brick and stone. She wondered how many eyes the windows held.

During the afternoon they had walked miles through the city because no tuk-tuk or taxi would give them a ride. Someone else seemed to have the same problem, but Sarah could never quite catch the person she sensed was following them. Eventually they had crossed the Howrah Bridge, by-passed the railway station, and entered an area she assumed was the infamous Howrah slum. By that time darkness had fallen and vanquished the malevolent stares of strangers that had accompanied them. Now she felt the night hid something worse.

"I was in a city of noise and movement," she said, "a city that pulsed with actuations. Now I'm on another planet. Where are you? Still teaching English at Calcutta University? Still wondering why they sacked you when your blood turned bad? And why your wife and kids left you when you ran out of money and got kicked out your house? Still wondering where the fuck we are? You're lost - admit it!"

Swami pushed himself up from against a wall. "I don't fully understand you. You are enigmatic. Come, we have rested enough from our long walk - and I am not lost. I once lived near here. I thought you would enjoy some sightseeing."

"Yeah, sure, fucking great." She looked around at the decrepitude. "We could have got a bus and saved a universe of time."

"You know I don't like buses. They carry too many people and they all stare at me...... when they let me on, that is."

"Let's go," Sarah urged. "I need Kali's sign. I could have jumped off the bridge into the river hours ago. This place stinks." She grimaced, turned, and walked away, unwholesome things squelching beneath her feet.

Swami trotted after her. "Follow me," and he overtook her.

"Follow him to sex and death," said the gruff voice.

Sarah banged the side of her head. "Go away," she

pleaded.

Swami looked over his shoulder. "I cannot. I feel responsible."

"Not you. The voice in my head."

"My seed would quieten it," he said suggestively.

"Don't listen to him!" the voice shouted. "The hump's a fucking parasite. His seed'll poison you with shit and pus and a million other festering filths he's got hidden in his stinking rotten system. Jesus Christ you're such a stupid little bitch at times."

The force of condemnation surprised Sarah and she checked in her pockets for the chlorpromazine tablets. Finding only a few tissues and banknotes she stopped, swore, and looked in her money belt.

"I've lost my pills," she shouted, nerves tightening. She looked around in a futile gesture. "Shit. They could be anywhere."

"Tablets for what?"

"For my problem, my head - shit! I've just remembered. I left them in my hotel room."

"Then we must make haste, and find the sign from Kali before your problem worsens," and Swami carried on into a maze of alleyways, Sarah trailing, negative thoughts clustering in her mind. Behind them shadowed eyes tracked their movements, footfalls silent in their wake.

They came out into a wide street shrouded in a night devoid of streetlamps or glowing windows. Anonymous buildings loomed over the dispossessed sleeping on old beds and planks, crates and paper. Their snores and rattling phlegm resounded in Sarah's ears like a sudden burst of warfare, and the darkness shifted shades every time she peered into it. A woman to her left shouted out in a native tongue.

"Ignore her," whispered Swami as they passed. "She's crazy."

The woman's shouting continued, growing louder. A male

voice joined in, then others. Sarah looked over her shoulder in an attempt to place them, saw several people spill out from a large doorway. Those waking along the street jumped up and joined them.

"I think they're going to follow us," she said.

The crowd surged towards them as two cars entered the street from either end, their headlights furrowing the darkness.

"Quick, down here." Swami grabbed her arm, pulled her down a narrow passage that stank of urine. "Run!" he ordered.

Behind them the street dwellers gathered speed, their number swollen by men they feared, some with radios. A small foreign woman, dishevelled and wild, reached the passage before them. They flowed after her like water down a conduit.

Swami turned left down another passage, then right, and slowed at a broken fence. "Through here," and he was gone.

Sarah darted after him, stumbling and cursing as weed-hidden masonry tore skin from her shins. She saw him jump a low wall like an antelope, too agile for a mass of deformity, she thought. She followed him over, rolled down an embankment, landed on a sacred cow that lurched to its feet with a stupified moan. Glancing up at the wall she saw two men and a woman coming over it.

Swami tugged her arm. "Quick quick. Not far now."

They ran across a road, down another flanked by warehouses, security lights adding a jaundiced pallor to the night. Swami veered to the left, vanished into darkness. Sarah followed, found herself inside a derelict warehouse. They climbed a ladder to the floor above, walked gingerly across broken boards, eased through a smashed window to the roof. After a short pause to catch their breath, they crossed a rusting walkway to another roof, and jumped a narrow gap to a third that overlooked the Hooghly River.

Lights beckoned in all directions, and on the other side of the river shone the majority of Calcutta. To their left the

Howrah Bridge stretched like the grey skeleton of a huge beast.

"Why were they chasing us?" Sarah asked.

"To rob, rape or kill - who knows? Life is cheap everywhere, especially here. Come, we must go."

They climbed down an iron ladder, made their way to the river's edge through a series of short alleys. Swami finally stopped at a crumbling bathing ghat and sat down. Wide rough steps disappeared into bronze-brown water.

"I think we are safe now," he said.

Much to his amazement Sarah stripped off - it seemed the right thing to do - and walked down the steps. A gritty coldness enveloped her feet and legs, numbing their soreness. Taking a deep breath she launched into an easy breaststroke, until something resembling a turd brushed her face and freaked her out. In an untidy panic she swam back and stretched out beside her clothes. The night was warm, and Swami laid beside her, his eyes feasting on her nakedness, his mind full of lustful notions.

A few stars spared by cloud winked at them, and Sarah wondered which one beamed messages into her head. She tried to tune in but found only her voices.

"Go away and leave me in peace," she whispered.

"Get fucked and I'll go away," offered the gruff voice.

"Going away is nothing more than going to," observed the shrill one. "Sleep obliviously and escape the inevitable," it concluded.

Sarah turned to Swami. "Make love to me in my sleep."

He grinned, old teeth filling his mouth. "How beautiful."

"Not really. I just want the voices in my head to go away."

"And so they will."

She laid back, closed her eyes. "I'm going to try and sleep now."

He waited until her breathing was slow and shallow, then stripped off and moved over her, trembling nervously with a rare excitement. Before he could do anything her eyes opened.

"I'm not asleep yet. Besides, where's Kali?"

"She will come soon." He looked at the scar on her belly. "Is this the mark of Kali?"

"No. It's the mark of Caesarian. It's how they stole my baby."

"I see." He flicked an insect from his flaccid penis. "Did you know that Kali first appeared by the Hooghly River before Calcutta existed? That's why we are here."

"He's here because he's a dirty filthy bastard who should be shot," came a hoarse reply only Sarah could hear."

She pushed Swami away and sat up. "I've changed my mind."

"Whose mind?" came a shrill response.

Swami shoved her back down. "I'm sorry, but I don't think I can allow that. You've brought me this far, so it's only fair that you allow me some release."

"Go and have a wank instead, if you can get it hard enough."

Swami caught the tail end, said, "Yes, I am having a little trouble, but that's because I prefer the other hole. My wife's was a very tight fit." His penis began to stiffen. "I think you will enjoy it." He made a clumsy attempt to turn her over. "Please don't resist and make me angry."

"Fuck off you creep," and she grabbed his penis and yanked back the skin. He yelped and rolled off, making her laugh.

"I was gentle with you," he yelled, "and this is how you reward me - like my wife. You're all the same, you women." He moved closer, his countenance changing dramatically. "You'll pay dearly for this humiliation," and he silenced Sarah's laughter with a slap round the face, its impact filling her head with electric crackle.

Sarah fell back, saw Swami's face blend into the inky backdrop, the river recede into the sky. Piggy eyes merged into one as he leaned over and kissed her breasts, then repositioned himself. She felt detached with paralysis as he groped between her legs, the tip of his penis touching her thighs like a dry stick. When he told her to turn over she didn't move. Infuriated, he straddled her legs and squeezed her nipples. She winced.

"This is nothing to what you will feel later, you bloody woman."

Sarah gazed over his shoulder and smiled.

"What are you bloody smiling at?" and he squeezed harder.

"She comes."

Three-eyed Kali, now goddess of time and the saviour of the universe, rose up black-skinned behind Swami, brought two of her many arms over his head to both sides of his neck, and as goddess of death and destruction, began to choke the life out of him.

His hands went to his throat, seeking purchase on the knotted cord around his neck. His piggy eyes expanded. His face grew darker. When he convulsed with a rattling gurgle and left her, Sarah laughed, stopping only when he fell to one side and revealed her Kali - an ordinary man, with another: the two who had chased them over the wall.

The second man pulled out a knife. Sarah sat up. He kicked her back down, kept her there with a foot on her chest. His accomplice grabbed her arms, pulled them back, put a foot on each one and squatted. He flicked the cord around her neck and tightened it. She opened her mouth to scream but nothing came out.

The knifeman unfastened his trousers, stepped off her chest. He pushed her legs apart, pulled out his stiff penis, knelt before her. When the strangler leaned over her face to kiss her, her earlobes tingled. Expecting a transmission from the star signal, she heard instead a new voice, soft as silk, clear as crystal, undeniable as death.

"Kill these dogs who dress as men and eat white babies.

Kill these fathers of deceit. Kill them now."

The knifeman's fingers probed between her legs, his knife resting on her stomach. The strangler's lips pressed down on hers, his tongue seeking entry. She allowed it in, and when she felt it slide wetly around her mouth, bit down hard, teeth meeting in a wrench of muscle and blood as she clamped her legs shut on the knifeman's hand.

The strangler shot noisily back out of sight, releasing her arms. She reached for the knife, the knifeman beating her to it, freeing his other hand as she spat the severed tongue into his face. He yelled, fell back, blood in his eyes. Sarah sprung to her feet, all her voices chanting *kill kill kill* like a pack of demented demons. Snatching up a stone she slammed it into his head. The blow knocked him sideways and he staggered in a half-turn as she hit him again. With a growl he lashed out wildly and missed, allowing her to grab his knife arm with both hands. As they grappled he shouted for help that never came, his accomplice writhing on the ground clutching his lower face, blood pouring from his mouth.

With one hand still tight on his arm, Sarah grabbed his testicles and squeezed with all her strength. He screamed and tripped over his trousers. She fell on top of him, still squeezing, his agony the best sound she had ever heard: strong, clear, and wrought with a justice that invigorated her. When the knife fell from his grasp, she let go of his arm and went to grab it, but a white hand snatched it up.

Sarah released the man's testicles, sprung up, and as he rolled into a sobbing ball Melissa plunged the knife repeatedly into him until he laid still.

"You're mine," she said to Sarah.

Sarah stared warily at her. "Who are you?"

"You don't remember?"

"No."

"I was in Alan Raddick's office at Kingston when he had to interview you. You wouldn't let me stay because you wanted

155

him for yourself. Remember now?" She moved closer, the knife dripping.

Sarah had no idea what she was talking about, and told her so.

"Don't give me that you scheming whore. If it wasn't for you I wouldn't be here trying to save Alan - you're all fucking mad you know, your whole family. And it's all your fault."

Sarah stared balefully at her. Whoever she was she didn't like her. "What do you know about my baby?" she asked irritably.

"Don't use that tone of voice with me," Melissa shouted. "First you try and seduce Alan at the hospital, then you suck him into your wretched family, force him to come out here with your father looking for you, then because of that I have to come out with your fucking mother to make sure she or your father doesn't drop him in the shit, and because of all that I end up getting humiliated and hurt and it's all because of you."

Her exceedingly shrill finish pierced Sarah's brain, inflaming her mood. "Fuck off and leave me alone," she said dismissively.

Melissa shot forward, stabbed air as Sarah side-stepped and thumped her on the chin with a right hook. She landed on her rump, sat dazed as Sarah gazed dispassionately down at her. Eventually she looked up and frowned.

"You're mad," Sarah stated. "Mad and useless."

Melissa's hands groped at her sides for the knife. When she found it Sarah kicked her under the chin and knocked her out. Behind her the strangler made ugly noises and she walked over to him with the knife, pleasantly light-headed. He cowered before her, blood still oozing between his fingers. She squatted beside him and smiled.

"I'm going to stab you to death," she announced matter-of-factly. "One stab for me, one for my baby, one for every man who's used me, one for Dr Raddick, one for every friend I've lost, and.....yes, I'd better include my voices otherwise they'll give me a hard time. How many's that?"

The strangler coughed blood.

"How messy. And of course, I've just remembered, you can't speak English, or can you? Guess you can't speak anything now you tongueless piece of shit," and she kicked him furiously until her foot hurt.

She sat down and watched him as she made a calculation. Finally she said, "I've got to stab you eighty-four times, and I will, I promise."

But she broke her promise and finished on thirty-eight, then washed in the Hooghly, dressed, and stood on the bathing ghat looking east across the river. The sky was lilac-black, tainted with city illuminations. Dawn was on its way and Melissa was stirring. It was time to move on.

16

ULTIMA RATIO

Sarah walked up a riverside path towards Howrah Bridge. Kali had delivered once again, and that was nice. It was important that women looked out for each other. Even her pills didn't seem so important now. And it was funny how schizophrenia and Calcutta were so similar. She chuckled; her doctors back home would appreciate that observation.

A savage disturbance swept her thoughts away, and she spun round in alarm. A mob of street dwellers was running her way, armed with thick sticks of wood like baseball bats and yelling incomprehensibly. With a curse she turned and sprinted.

The path dipped and curved and went on and on, the mob falling silent behind her, their feet pounding a steady rhythm. Sarah doubled it, gained precious distance, Howrah Bridge slowly enlarging on the periphery of her vision. When the path curved sharply upwards she found herself running up wide never-ending steps, her calves and thighs solidifying, hot knives slipping between her ribs, the air she sucked in not seeming to reach her lungs.

Finally the steps did end, and Melissa was there with the knife to confirm it. She pounced as Sarah tripped over the top step and fell sideways, the blade missing by several inches. Before Sarah could think about defending herself, Mitra's Mercedes pulled up and Janet leapt out, shouting at Melissa to finish her off.

Sarah spat bile as Melissa screamed insults at her mother. Mitra got out and waved a pistol in the air. Janet started yelling at him. Melissa lunged at her and they wrestled over the knife. Mitra tried to separate them. The mob were almost at the top. Sarah got in the car, the engine still running, and scanned the controls. The pistol went off but no one seemed to be hit. She selected a gear, released the brake, reversed the car until it pointed diagonally at the steps. Mitra turned and shouted. Janet fell into him. Melissa stabbed her in the breast. Sarah changed gear and accelerated.

The car hit all three of them, smashed into a wall, teetered over the steps. Mitra and Janet tumbled down to the mob, immobile now as the Mercedes blocked the top and tilted in their direction. Sarah stared down at them, then looked at Melissa crushed into the wall. Only her head and shoulders were visible, and she stared lifelessly.

When Sarah jumped smartly out, the car immediately tilted away and began to roll sideways down the steps, the mob fleeing back down with cries of alarm. It rolled with a terrifying din that took the edge off her pleasure, but she nevertheless stood and watched as it rolled over her mother and Mitra, caught some of the mob, and then moved more untidily, suddenly exploding halfway down, flames engulfing stragglers.

"Watching is learning," she muttered to herself. She looked at Melissa lying face-down in a pool of blood. "Happy now?"

The only response was the faint sound of another car and more pounding feet. She looked up the road, cursed vehemently. Was there no end to this? With a final burst of energy she ran in the opposite direction, and soon met a few people running towards her. She was tempted to stop, but continued, determined to beat them out the way if necessary. It wasn't, and apart from the odd cursory glance they ignored her. The explosion, she realized belatedly, and slowed a little as she saw a large familiar building up ahead. Outside it were taxis and people with luggage, cloth bundles and baskets of produce. Praise the gods! Howrah station.

She increased her speed, collided with a taxi, bounced off

and sprawled breathlessly in the road. The driver jumped out, barked annoyingly. Sarah got up, saw the other car closing in, men running behind it. Turning to the taxi driver she pulled out her banknotes, ordered him to take her to Chowringhee whatever the cost.

The few seconds it took him to nod seemed like an hour, and as he got behind the wheel Sarah dived in the back, the taxi enclosing her like a womb. A quick U-turn and they were off, the pursuing car right behind them, its accompanying men now demons staring with amber eyes, curved teeth extending from their jaws, their hands turning to claws ready to rip them apart.

"Drive drive DRIVE!" Sarah screamed.

The driver accelerated as a demon tried to cut them off and threw himself at the back window. Sarah twisted, punched the glass. The driver glanced anxiously over his shoulder. The taxi swerved, the demon fell off, another took his place then lost his grip as the taxi gained speed, shot blindly into the main road and swung right to the bridge.

"They were doggin' the flash out my pram with a spoon of jack to lift their thoughts," gushed Sarah panting and shaking, her mind bursting chaotically with voices and wild notions. "Crazy bastards. They won't fool me." She slumped back and closed her eyes.

The driver shot her a quizzical look as Howrah Bridge rose like a leviathan around them, its stark grey construction blending with the dirty dawn sky. Trucks thundered along its worn backbone with blaring horns. Old black cars belched fumes. Tuks-tuks weaved dangerously in and out. Mopeds diced with death.

Sarah looked out the back window. The car was still behind them, the demons inside misting its windows with desire. A tuk-tuk swung out from behind a truck following the car, and crept along its flank. Another came in its wake. She watched as they edged in behind the car like wasps inspecting sweet fruit. Men leaned out the sides and stared in her direction.

"It's them!" she cried.

The driver checked his mirror, muttered and left the bridge, sweeping round towards Chowringhee, his hand on the horn. The tuks-tuks grew distant but the car remained. The taxi sped on. Sarah fell into fantasy, the driver into profound unease, his eyes moving from road to mirror to Sarah in a constant cycle until at the northern end of the Maidan a loud crash flung them forwards, another following seconds later.

The taxi had hit a bus. And the pursuing car had hit the taxi.

Sarah staggered out, a bewildering cacophony filling her head. She caught snatches of the taxi driver yelling at the bus driver, Dua yelling at them both, the bus driver yelling back, his passengers yelling at all three of them, other vehicles snarling around the scene like ravenous beasts. The taxi driver tried to stop her, screaming for his fare. The bus driver grabbed him, thinking he was trying to flee the accident. Bill clambered towards Sarah, calling her name. Someone whose car he climbed over demanded money. The taxi driver added his demand. The bus driver shook him by the throat. Raddick followed Bill. Dua followed Raddick. The taxi driver punched the bus driver and chased after Dua. The bus driver chased the taxi driver. Crowds clustered. Sarah's voices shrieked. Dirty air invaded her pores. She fought for freedom with anonymous hands, hurled insults at walls of brown faces, found space and ran ran ran, Bill on her heels, Raddick close behind him, then Dua and the drivers.

Down Red Road. Into the Maidan. Cutting east, her voices screaming conflicting orders, insults, nonsense, leading her nowhere until chance led her to Nehru Road and Bill burst his lungs with a final surge and clipped her heels. They fell in the road, vehicles bearing down, horns blaring, brakes screeching, the distance too short. Sarah scrabbled away, truck wheels brushing her legs as she pulled herself over a kerb, heard a screaming crunch and rolled on to the pavement, oblivious to what had happened.

Faces came and went like yo-yos on legs of string. The sky washed her face with dishwater. The pavement shook. Buildings oscillated. Her ears burned with noise. She got to her feet, pushed through gathering scarecrows and trotted off, a pile of builders' rubble alerting her to the existence of Sudder Street. Sure that safety was close, she ran faster, passing loinclothed men washing under a street tap, a shrivelled old woman encamped with four mangy dogs beside a Salvation Army Hostel, a child playing with a - .

Sarah stopped abruptly.

Turned.

Marched back and kicked the old woman's cardboard shelter to pieces, screaming at the dogs as she kicked them all over the pavement until they fled and the old woman was left dazed in the gutter. Then back down the street to an alfresco chay shop on the corner of Stuart Lane, where men sat on the kerb drinking tea and watching her, and down the lane to the Paragon Hotel, and beyond it, to a snake charmer in a yellow turban sitting on dirty concrete arranging his snake sacks around him, releasing a pair of cobras, making ready with his pipe until Sarah yanked his turban off, beat him round the head, kicked his snakes and sacks all over the lane, and before he could gather his senses, took off into the hotel.

While the snake charmer chased his cobras, Sarah marched wildly through the eating area full of travellers having breakfast, snatching food from their plates and babbling incoherently until she reached a familiar corridor, ran down it, and kicked open the door to room 14, splintering the frame, alarming the staff.

Three young men came to investigate, found her ransacking the room, the bed already overturned, money hidden beneath the mattress now safely in her money belt, her attentions focused on the search for something she couldn't remember.

She swept clothes and more money into her travelling bag, upended a small table, raged around the room cursing and shouting, and finally stopped, turned to the three in the doorway with a face like a hyena wearing a nose stud, and said, "Where's my plastic bastards you retching pills?"

One of them looked at something on the floor. Sarah saw what and grabbed it, unscrewed the top and gulped down four tablets.

When the three began an angry outburst and moved towards her, she picked up her bag and leapt at them with a snarl. They jumped back as she stormed out down the corridor, through the eating area and into reception. She deposited a few banknotes on the counter, glared at those behind her with eyes as sharp as broken bottles, and emerged into sunlight. When the snake charmer saw her he shouted and hurried towards her, then changed his mind and retreated.

She walked for ten minutes before briefly consulting her map. The pills were beginning to have a slight effect. Even so, too much had happened and she couldn't clearly remember what, only that millions of people had invaded her mind and body space and she had to get out. If she stayed they'd invade her for good and she'd never get away.

In a flash she decided: Sealdah railway station for the train to Bangaon on the border with Bangladesh. It made sense: she had a passport and Sealdah had lines running in the right direction. She saw a tuk-tuk down the road, chased after it, climbed in, pointed to her destination on the map, and laughed wildly as the vehicle shuddered and pulled away.

17

CATCHING THE CYCLONE

Raddick held Bill's head, blood pooling around them.

"Where's the ambulance?" he shouted at Dua, but he knew it was too late. The truck had crushed Bill's pelvis and lower abdomen, and life was leaving him; he could see it in his eyes.

Bill blinked, mumbled something. Raddick moved his ear over Bill's mouth, tried to block out the background hubbub.

"Cold...can't feel."

"The ambulance is on its way. Save your strength, don't talk." He rearranged Dua's jacket over him.

"Listen," Bill murmured. "Listen."

"I'm listening."

"Sarah....had boy...Feb'ry." Something caught in his throat and Raddick lifted his head higher. "False...adoption....Janet's plan."

"Where is he?"

"Roger...Judith...Armstrong...six..teen." He coughed, eyes glazing.

"Come on Bill, hang on, speak to me - for Sarah's sake."

Bill breathed sporadically. "Molson Av'nue...Epsom. Take it...give Sarah....look after her....Janet...me...dead...Sarah get everything. Promise me...you make her well.....promise..."

"I promise, Bill. Don't worry, I'll get the baby back and look after them both." He stroked Bill's cheek for no obvious reason. "I'll make it my mission in life." And for a strange moment he had a feeling that he would.

"Go...find Sarah."

"I'll find her, don't worry."

Bill said nothing more.

Sarah boarded the train as police officers arrived in Sudder Street to question locals and check hotels for a crazy foreign girl suspected of murder and theft. As the half-empty electric train pulled out, Raddick and Dua entered the Paragon Hotel ahead of the police and questioned the staff. Within minutes they were casting their net further afield.

By the time Sarah arrived in Bangaon, three hours later, she was feeling calm and self-assured. She passed through the Indian exit procedure without problem, and on the Bangladeshi side of the border, a sleek diamond-eyed woman in military green and pressed khaki examined her passport with deliberate slowness. When a telephone rang before she completed her examination, she went into a spartan back office to answer it, taking the passport with her.

Sarah listened, unable to understand a word the woman was saying. Bored, she sat on a chair and waited as she finished the call and made one of her own. A minute later two men entered the office and stood by the door. Their uniforms were similar to the woman's, but unlike her they carried pistols in holsters, the flaps open. They stared at Sarah with curious expressions, and when she smiled at them, they smiled back.

The woman returned, and ignoring the men resumed her examination of the passport. With a shake of her head she handed it back.

"No entry visa for Bangladesh," she stated.

"I thought I could get one here."

"No. At embassy only."

"Where's that?"

"Delhi, maybe Calcutta."

Sarah puckered her lips. This was news she didn't want to hear. She picked up her bag. "Will the Indians let me back in?"

The woman's eyes flashed with a secret amusement.

"I think so."

When Sarah left the office, the two men followed her to the Indian border control, then returned. A man sitting behind a battered desk took her passport, stamped it, gave it back without a word. Somehow it all seemed too easy. As soon as she stepped outside the building she found out why.

Two burly policemen grabbed her arms, lifted her off the ground. A third took her bag. Before she could react, a familiar face appeared before her and smiled.

"Hi Sarah. Remember me?"

Her eyes narrowed suspiciously. "Dr. Raddick?"

"Yes. I've come to help you."

Her feet re-established contact with the ground. "You've changed."

"Yes, I have. Would you like to change, too?"

"Maybe. Why?"

"I want to take you home."

"I don't want to go home," and she began to struggle.

"That's where your baby boy is."

She ceased moving and frowned. "Oxshott?"

"No. Epsom. A couple are looking after him. If you want him back you're going to have to sort yourself out. Will you let me help you do that, so you can be reunited with him?" His words didn't seem to register, and he said, "Do you understand me, Sarah?"

"Yes, of course I do."

"And you'll let me help you with your medication and rehabilitation, and everything else?"

"Yes, anything. I just want my baby back. They stole it from me, you know. Can you imagine that? And everyone thought I was mad, making it up like some paranoid fool, but it was my parents - my mother, all her doing."

"She's dead, Sarah."

"I know. I saw it happen."

Raddick moved closer, his voice softer. "And so is your

father. He was run over soon after your taxi crashed, when he was - ."

There was no point in saying more. She didn't need that sort of guilt. It would only gnaw away at her over the years and do her harm, and Bill wouldn't have wanted that.

"Was he chasing me?" she asked.

Oh shit, thought Raddick, summoning his resolve. "No. He was just unlucky. Misjudged the distance and speed. I'm sorry."

She looked sad for a moment, as. if remembering her father from happier times. "We all turn to dust at the end," she said. She glanced at the policemen either side of her. "Can you ask them to let me go?"

"Yes, but first, do we have a deal - my help in return for you helping yourself?"

"Yes."

"You sure?"

"Yes."

"Have you taken any of your medicine since Calcutta?"

"I took four chlorpromazine pills before getting on the train."

"How do you feel now?"

"Bit tired, but okay."

Raddick looked at the policemen. "You can let her go now."

As they released her, he held out his hand. Sarah took it and they walked to a car parked behind a police jeep. Dua got out and nodded solemnly at her.

"Where are we going?" she asked.

"The airport," Raddick replied.

"I've got enough money for the tickets," she said helpfully.

"Really?"

"Oh yes. I've still got about ten thousand pounds left, maybe more."

Raddick looked at the policeman carrying her bag,

gestured for him to hand it over. He ignored Raddick, but when Sarah got in the back of the car, he placed it on her lap.

Raddick stuck his head in, said, "I've just got to give the driver directions, then we'll go."

He moved off to the jeep, beckoned Dua over.

"She seems settled at the moment. Have you fixed everything with the police?"

"Yes. They think Mitra and his gang were trying to kidnap Sarah in order to extract a ransom from her parents, but the plan went terribly wrong. I have explained that Sarah is very ill, and the tragic events have made her worse, and that as her doctor you must take her back to England for treatment. As for the deaths by the river, they have been attributed to Mitra's lot. The young woman - Melissa Burnham - is viewed as an innocent bystander who tried to help but got more than she bargained for. Do you wish her body to be flown to England with the Donaldsons?"

"No. Let the British Embassy sort that out."

"Is Sarah aware of what has happened to her parents?"

"Sort of. I'll talk to her more fully about them later on, when I've got her on a proper course of treatment. Is the Lear ready to roll?"

"It has been on stand-by since the day we arrived. I telephoned my Delhi office while you were waiting for Sarah to cross back over the border, and they confirmed that a larger aircraft has been chartered for your flight from Delhi to London. The arrangements were backdated and the cost and other expenses spread around Mr. Donaldson's credit cards, as we agreed. Copying his signature presented no problem, nor the amount of the transactions. It seems his credit card companies often see large amounts of money on his accounts."

"They won't any more."

"No, his death is most tragic."

"Yes." Raddick recalled Bill's final seconds. It had taken

the last of his strength to utter those all-important words. It had been the only thing left he could do to help Sarah and make amends, and he'd cut it so fine he could have died without shedding any light on her baby. The thought was unnerving. "Is there anything else, Mr Dua?"

"A few minor loose ends, but nothing you need worry about. I shall deal with them in due course. In fact, I think we should go now. The police officers are growing impatient."

Janet and Bill were cremated eight days after Raddick and Sarah arrived back in England. Reuniting Sarah with her baby took longer.

Raddick gave her a choice: they could either contact the police and get bogged down in the justice system - which he didn't recommend - or wait until her parents' affairs had been sorted out, then simply snatch the baby and disappear abroad.

Sarah suggested snatching the baby immediately and clearing off to anywhere nice. Raddick explained to her why that wasn't such a good idea, especially as she'd contracted hepatitis while in India and hadn't completed the first stage of his rehabilitative treatment. Thanks to the hepatitis laying her out for several weeks, plus a bit of mild sedation thrown in for good measure, he eventually got his own way.

Within a few months most of Janet's estate had been sorted out and transferred to Sarah, and expediting matters with cash payments ensured that most of Bill's more complicated affairs were completed a couple of months after that. By this time Sarah had fully recovered from the hepatitis, and with her mental faculties more in order, was growing increasingly impatient. Aware that he couldn't delay matters any longer, Raddick planned accordingly. He and Sarah changed their names by deed poll and obtained all the necessary documentation they would need to travel abroad.

Sarah's son was snatched from Judith Armstrong's car while she spoke to another driver who had clipped her wing.

The car was stolen, the driver in it for £1,000. Three hours later the baby (renamed) was flying first class to Canada with Christina and Charles Whittington - Sarah and Raddick - between them worth £3.75 million pounds, a quarter of it in joint bank accounts, most of it having been realized from the sale of Bill's corporate and property assets. Five days later they took up residence at a five-acre estate on a remote part of Costa Rica's unspoilt coastline, and wondered how they were ever going to spend the interest generated by their investments.

Sarah progressed rapidly under her husband's care, the baby and new environment contributing enormously. Within a couple of months her medication virtually ceased, and encouraged by Raddick she resumed her creative activities: he thought they would act as a good indicator to her mental state. He didn't want her falling ill again prematurely.

As for Raddick, he spent his time attending to the estate, reading and writing, accessing the internet, and planning for the future. Life for him could have been so much worse, and now it looked like it was going to get infinitely better.

And so it continued, idyllic in most ways, until one balmy night Raddick fell asleep earlier than normal. He had eaten a curry made by Sarah. It had been heavily laced with a benzodiazepine usually used to treat insomnia. As he slept, Sarah stabbed him. To death. Then she buried him in the easily dug soil by the driveway, and planted some shrubs in case she forgot where she'd buried him. Hard work but worth it, and in bed with baby by three in the morning.

Murder is a callous way to deal with a good samaritan, but Sarah was damned sure she knew what Raddick had been up to. Oh yes, despite the illness and drugs, she knew. The signs were everywhere.

He wanted to get his hands on all her money and then dump her in some godforsaken lunatic asylum without her baby.

No way. Him or anyone else. No way. *Ever*.

Cover design by the author.

The two scenes on the front depict riverside activity along the River Ganges in Varanasi. In the top photo, the body of a holy man wrapped in cloth and tied to a stretcher bobs about near men cleaning kitchen utensils. In the bottom picture a sacred cow rots at the foot of steps leading to nowhere in particular.

The back photo is a snake charmer (pretty obvious, eh?) caught in Stuart Lane, off Sudder Street, Calcutta, just before Sarah messed up his act.